SACRAMENTO PUBLIC LIBRARY

W9-CZD-400

NHI fic
14
Spencer, El The light in the pi
McGraw-Hill 1960
3 3029 00413 6461

5/96 CIR 2.

fic cop
5/73

Spencer, Elizabeth.

The light in the
piazza

WITHDRAWN FROM COLLECTION
OF SACRAMENTO PUBLIC LIBRARY

DATE			

88   NORTH HIGHLANDS

78   © THE BAKER & TAYLOR CO.

THE LIGHT IN THE PIAZZA

THE
LIGHT IN THE

New York   London   Toronto

PIAZZA

ELIZABETH
SPENCER

McGraw-Hill Book Company, Inc.

THE LIGHT IN THE PIAZZA
Copyright © 1960 by Elizabeth Spencer.
Printed in the United States of America.
All rights reserved. This book or parts
thereof may not be reproduced in any form
without written permission of the publishers.

Most of the material in this book originally
appeared in *The New Yorker* in somewhat
different form.

Library of Congress Catalog Card Number: 60-15005

First Edition
Sixth Printing

60190

All names, characters, and events in this book are
fictional; any seeming resemblance to actual persons,
living or dead, is therefore purely coincidental.

NORTH HIGHLANDS

c. 14

To John

THE LIGHT IN THE PIAZZA

*Setting —
Locality Abercroft?
modern time & to Cam*

i

ON A JUNE AFTERNOON at sunset, an American woman and
her daughter fended their way along a crowded street in
Florence and entered with relief the spacious Piazza della
Signoria. They were tired from a day of tramping about
with a guidebook, often in the sun. The cafe that faced the
Palazzo Vecchio was a favorite spot for them; without dis-
cussion they sank down at an empty table. The Florentines
seemed to favor other gathering places at this hour. No cars
were allowed here, though an occasional bicycle skimmed
through; and a few people, passing, met in little knots of
conversation, then dispersed. A couple of tired German tourists, all but harnessed in fine camera equipment, sat at the

foot of Cellini's triumphant Perseus, slumped and staring at nothing.

Margaret Johnson, lighting a cigarette, relaxed over her apéritif and regarded the scene which she preferred before any other, anywhere. She never got enough of it, and now in the clear evening light that all the shadows had gone from —the sun being blocked away by the tight bulk of the city—she looked at the splendid old palace and forgot that her feet hurt. More than that: here she could almost lose the sorrow that for so many years had been a constant of her life. About the crenellated tower where the bells hung, a few swallows darted.

Margaret Johnson's daughter Clara looked up from the straw of her orangeade. She too seemed quieted from the fretful mood to which the long day had reduced her. "What happened here, Mother?"

"Well, the statue over there, the tall white boy, is by Michelangelo. You remember him. Then—though it isn't a very happy thought—there was a man burned to death right over there, a monk."

Any story attracted her. "Why was he burned?"

"Well, he was a preacher who told them they were wicked and they didn't like him for it. People were apt to be very cruel in those days. It all happened a long while ago. They must feel sorry about it because they put down a marker to his memory."

Clara jumped up. "I want to see!" She was off before her mother could restrain her. For once Margaret Johnson thought, Why bother? In truth the space before them, so satisfyingly wide, like a pasture, might tempt any child to run across it. To Margaret Johnson, through long habit, it came naturally now to think like a child. Clara, she now saw, running with her head down to look for the marker, had bumped squarely into a young Italian. There went the straw hat she had bought in Fiesole. It sailed off prettily, its broad red ribbon a quick mark in the air. The young man was after it; he contrived to knock it still further away, once and again, though the day was windless; his final success was heroic. Now he was returning, smiling, too graceful to be true; they were all too graceful to be true. Clara was talking to him. She pointed back toward her mother. Oh Lord! He was coming back with Clara.

Margaret Johnson, confronted at close range by two such radiant young faces, was careful not to produce a very cordial smile.

"We met him before, Mother. Don't you remember?"

She didn't. They all looked like carbon copies of each other.

He gave a suggestion of a bow. "My—store—" English was coming out. "It—is—near—Piazza della Repubblica —how do you say? The beeg square. Oh yes, and on Sunday, si fanno la musica. Museek, bom, bom." He was a whole orchestra, though his gestures were small. "And the lady—" Now a busty Neapolitan soprano sprang to view, in pink lace, one hand clenched to her heart. Margaret Johnson could not help laughing. Clara was delighted.

Ah, he had pleased. He dropped the role at once. "My store—is there." A chair was vacant. "Please?" He sat.

Here came the inevitable card. They were shoppers, after all, or would be. Well, it was better than compliments, offers to guide them, thought Mrs. Johnson. She took the card. It was in English except for the unpronounceable name. "Via Strozzi 8," she read. "Ties. Borsalino Hats. Gloves. Handkerchiefs. Everything for the Gentlemens."

"Not for you. But for your husband," he said to Mrs. Johnson. In these phrases he was perfectly at home.

"He isn't here, unfortunately."

"Ah, but you must take him presents. Excuse me." Now Clara was given a card. "And for your husband also."

She giggled. "I don't have a husband!"

"Signorina! Ah! Forgive me." He touched his breast. Again the quick suggestion of a bow. "Fabrizio Naccarelli." It sounded like a whole aria.

"I'm Clara Johnson," the girl said at once. Mrs. Johnson closed her eyes.

"Jean—Jean—" He strained for it.

"No, *John*son."

"Ah! Van Johnson!"

"That's right!"

"He is—cugino—parente—famiglia—?"

"No," said Mrs. Johnson irritably. She prided herself on her tolerance and interest among foreigners, but she was tired and Italians are so inquisitive. Given ten words of English, they will invent a hundred questions from them. This one at least was sensitive. He withdrew at once. "Clara," he said, as if to himself. No trouble there. The girl gave him her innocent smile.

14

Indeed, she could be remarkably lovely when pleased. The somewhat long lines of her cheek and jaw drooped when she was downhearted, but happiness drew her up perfectly. Her dark blue eyes grew serene and clear; her chestnut hair in its long girlish cut shadowed her smooth skin.

Due to an accident years ago, she had the mental age of a child of ten. But anyone on earth, meeting her for the first time, would have found this incredible. Mrs. Johnson had managed in many tactful ways to explain her daughter to young men without wounding them. She could even keep them from feeling too sorry for herself. "Every mother in some way wants a little girl who never grows up. Taken in that light, I do often feel fortunate. She is remarkably sweet, you see, and I find her a great satisfaction." She did not foresee any such necessity with an Italian out principally to sell everything for the gentlemens. No, he could not offer them anything else. No, he certainly could not pay the check. He had been very kind . . . very kind . . . yes, yes, very, very kind. . . .

Fabrizo

Clara ~~daughter~~ daughter

MRS Jhonson (Marget)

ii

BUT FABRIZIO NACCARELLI, whether Margaret Johnson had cared to master his name or not, was not one to be underestimated. He was very much at home in Florence where he had been born and his father before him and so on straight back to the misty days before the Medici, and he had given, besides, some little attention to the ways of the stranieri who were always coming to his home town. It seemed in the next few days that he showed up on every street corner. Surely he could not have counted so much on the tie they might decide to buy for Signor Johnson.

Clara invariably lighted up when they saw him, and he in turn communicated over and over his innocent pleasure in this happiest of coincidences. Mrs. Johnson noted that at each encounter he managed to extract from them some new piece of information, foremost among them, How long would they remain? Caught between two necessities, that of lying to him and not lying to her daughter, she revealed that the date was uncertain and saw the flicker of triumph in his eyes. And the next time they met—well, it was too much. By then they were friends. Could he offer them dinner that evening? He knew a place only for Florentines—good, good, very good. "Oh, yes!" said Clara. Mrs. Johnson demurred. He was very kind, but in the evenings they were always too tired. She was drawing Clara away in a pretense of hurry. The museum might close at noon. At the mention of noon the city bells began clanging all around them. It was difficult to hear. "In the Piazza," he cried in farewell, with a gesture toward the Piazza della Signoria, smiling at Clara, who waved her hand, though Mrs. Johnson went on saying, "No, we can't," and shaking her head.

Late that afternoon, they were taking a cup of tea in the big casino near Piazzale Michelangelo when Clara looked at her watch and said they must go.

"Oh, let's stay a little while longer and watch the sun set," her mother suggested.

"But we have to meet Fabrizio." The odd name came naturally to her tongue.

"Darling, Fabrizio will probably be busy until very late."

It was always hard for Mrs. Johnson to face the troubling-over of her daughter's wide, imploring eyes. Perhaps she should make some pretense, though pretense was the very thing she had constantly to guard against. The doctors had been very firm with her here. As hard as it was to be the source of disappointment, such decisions had to be made. They must be communicated, tactfully, patiently, reasonably. Clara must never feel that she had been deceived. Her whole personality might become confused. Mrs. Johnson sighed, remembering all this, and began her task.

"Fabrizio will understand if we do not come, Clara, because I told him this morning we could not. You remember that I did? I told him that because I don't think we should make friends with him."

"Why?"

"Because he has his own life here and he will stay here always. But we must go away. We have to go back home and see Daddy and Brother and Ronnie—" Ronnie was Clara's collie dog—"and Auntie and all the others. You know how hard it was to leave Ronnie even though you were coming back? Well, it would be very hard to like Fabrizio, wouldn't it, and leave him and never come back at all?"

"But I already like him," said Clara. "I could write him letters," she added wistfully.

"Things are often hard," said Mrs. Johnson, in her most cheery and encouraging tone.

It seemed a crucial evening. She did not trust Fabrizio not to call for them at their hotel, or doubt for a moment that he had informed himself exactly where they were staying. So she was careful before dinner to steer Clara to that other piazza—not the Signoria—once the closing hour for the shops had passed. Secure in the pushing crowds of Florentines, she chose one of the less fashionable cafes, settling at a corner table behind a green hedge which grew out of boxes and over the top of which there presently appeared the face of Fabrizio.

She saw him first in Clara's eyes. Next he was beaming upon them. There had been a mistake, of course. He had said only piazza piazza. How could they know? Difficile. He was so sorry. Pardon, pardon.

There was simply nothing to be gained by trying to stare him down. His great eyes showed concern, relief, gaiety as clearly as if the words had been written on them, but self-betrayal was unknown to him. Trying to surprise him at his game, one grew distracted and became aware how beautiful his eyes were. His dress gave him away if anything did. Nothing could be neater, cleaner, more carefully or sleekly tailored. His shirt was starched and white; his black hair still gleamed faintly damp at the edges; his close-cut, cuffless gray trousers ended in new black shoes of a pebbly leather with pointed toes. A faint whiff of cologne seemed to come from him. There was something too much here, and a little touching. Well, they would be leaving soon, thought Mrs. Johnson. She decided to relax and enjoy the evening.

But more than this was in it.

When she finally sat back from her excellent meal, lighting a cigarette and setting down her little cup of coffee, she glanced from the distance of her age toward the two young people. It was an advantage that Clara knew no Italian. She smiled sweetly and laughed innocently, so how was Fabrizio to know her dreary secret? Now Clara had taken out all her store of coins, the aluminum five- and ten-lire pieces that amused her, and was setting them on the table in little groups, pyramids and squares and triangles. Fabrizio, his handsome cheek leaning against his palm, was helping her with the tip of one finger, setting now this one, now that one, in place. They looked like two children, thought Mrs. Johnson.

It was as if a curtain had lifted before her eyes. The life she had thought forever closed to her daughter spread out its great pastoral vista.

After all, she thought, why not?

ѕᴇ, the whole idea was absurd. She remem-
ᴄᴇ when she woke the next morning, and
t have had too much wine, she thought.

: must leave for Rome in a day or two," said

ᴏ., ᴍᴏᴛᴍᴇʀ!" Clara's face fell.

It was a mistake to set her brooding on a bad day. The
rain which had started with a rumble of thunder in the early
morning hours was splashing down on the stone city. From
their window a curtain of gray hung over the river, dimming
the outlines of buildings on the opposite bank. The carrozza
drivers huddled in chilly bird shapes under their great black
umbrellas; the horses stood in crook-legged misery; and

metaphor 23

water streamed down all the statues. Mrs. Johnson and Clara put on sweaters and went downstairs to the lobby, where Clara was persuaded to write postcards. Once started, the task absorbed her. The selection of which picture for whom, the careful printing of the short sentences. Even Ronnie must have the card picked especially for him, a statue of a Roman dog. Toward lunch time the sun broke out beautifully. Clara knew the instant it did and startled her mother, who was looking through a magazine.

"It's quit raining!"

Mrs. Johnson was quick. "Yes, and I think if it gets hot again in the afternoon we should go up to the big park and take a swim. You know how you love to swim and I miss it too. Wouldn't that be fun?"

She had her difficulties, but when they had walked a short way along streets that were misty from the drying rain, had eaten in a small restaurant, but seen no sign of anyone they knew, Clara was persuaded.

Mrs. Johnson enjoyed the afternoon. The park had been refreshed by the rain, and the sun sparkled hot and bright on the pool. They swam and bought ice cream on sticks from the vender, and everyone smiled at them, obviously acknowledging a good sight. Mrs. Johnson, though blonde, had the kind of skin that never quite lost the good tan she had once given it, and her figure retained its trim firmness. She showed what she was: the busy American housewife, mother, hostess, cook, and civic leader, who paid attention to her looks. She sat on a bench near the pool, drying in the sun, smoking, her smart beach bag open beside her, watching her

similar/varite

daughter, who swam like a fish, flashing here and there in the pool. She plucked idly at the wet ends of her hair and wondered if she needed another rinse. She observed without the slightest surprise the head and shoulders of Fabrizio surfacing below the diving board, as though he had been swimming under water the entire time since they had arrived.

Like most Italians he was proud of his body and, having ance, lost no time in getting out of the truth slightly bowlegged, but he concealed ing in partial profile with one knee bent. t Mrs. Johnson, it was just too much for d them splash water in each other's faces, ush Fabrizio into the pool, Fabrizio pretend to the pool, Clara chase Fabrizio out among down the fall of ground nearby. Endlessly flitted like butterflies through the sunlight. Except that terflies, thought Mrs. Johnson, do not really think very much about sex. The final thing that had happened at home, that had really decided them on another trip abroad, was that Clara had run out one day and flung her arms around the grocery boy.

These problems had been faced, they had been reasoned about, patiently explained; it was understood what one did and didn't do to be good. But impulse is innocent about what is good or bad. A scar on the right side of her daughter's head, hidden by hair, lingered, shaped like the new moon. It was where her Shetland pony, cropping grass, had kicked in a temper at whatever was annoying him. Mrs.

25

Johnson had been looking through the window, and she still remembered the silence that had followed her daughter's sidelong fall, more heart-numbing than any possible cry.

Things would certainly take care of themselves sooner or later, Mrs. Johnson assured herself. She had seen the puzzled look commence on many a face and had begun the weary maneuvering to see yet another person alone before the next meeting with Clara. Right now, for instance—Clara could never play for long without growing hysterical, screaming even. There, she had almost tripped Fabrizio; he had done an exaggerated flip in the air. She collapsed into laughter, gasping, her two hands thrust to her face in a spasm. Poor child, thought her mother. But then Fabrizio came to her and took her hands down. In one quick motion he stood her straight and she grew quiet. Something turned over in Mrs. Johnson's breast.

They stood before her, panting, their sun-dried skin like so much velvet. "Look," cried Clara, and parted the hair above her ear. "I have a scar over my ear!" She pointed. "A scar. See!"   scar -scicatvr?

Fabrizio struck down her hand and put her hair straight. "No. Ma sono belli. Your hair—is beautiful."

We must certainly leave for Rome tomorrow, Mrs. Johnson thought. She heard herself thinking it, at some distance, as though in a dream.

She entered thus from that day a conscious duality of existence, knowing what she should and must do and making no motion toward doing it. The Latin temperament may

26

thrive on such subtleties and never find it necessary to conclude them, but to Mrs. Johnson the experience was strange and new. It confused her. She believed, as most Anglo-Saxons do, that she always acted logically and to the best of her ability on whatever she knew to be true. And now she found this quality immobilized and all her actions taken over by the simple drift of the days.

She had, in fact, come face to face with Italy.

iv

SOMETHING SURELY would arise to help her.

One had only to sit still while Fabrizio—he of the endless resource—outgeneraled himself and so caught on, or until he tired of them and dreamed of something else. One had only to make sure that Clara went nowhere alone with him. The girl had not a rebellious bone in her, and under her mother's eye she could be kept in tune.

But if Mrs. Johnson had been consciously striving to make a match, she could not have discovered a better line to take. Fabrizio's father was Florentine, but his mother was a Neapolitan, who went regularly to mass and was suspicious of foreigners. She received with approval the news that the piccola signorina americana was not allowed to so much as mail a postcard without her mother along. "Ma sono italiane? Are they Italian?" she wanted to know. "No, Mamma, non credo." And though Fabrizio declaimed his grand impatience with the signora americana, in his heart he was pleased.

A few days later, to the immense surprise of Fabrizio, who was taking coffee with the ladies in the big piazza, they happened to be noticed by an Italian gentleman, rather broad in girth, with a high-bridged Florentine nose and a pair of close-set, keen, cold eyes. "Ah, Papà!" cried Fabrizio. "Fortuna! Signora, signorina, permette. My father."

Signor Naccarelli spoke English very well indeed. Yes, it was a bit rusty perhaps, he must apologize. He had known many Americans during the war, had done certain small things for them in liaison during the occupation. He had found them very simpatici, quite unlike the Germans, whom he detested.

This was a set speech. It gave him time. His face was not at all regular; the jaw went sideways from his high forehead, and his mouth, like Fabrizio's, was somewhat thin. But his eye was pale, and he and Mrs. Johnson did not waste time in taking each other's measure. She sensed his intelligence at once. Now at last, she thought ruefully, between disappointment and relief, the game would be up.

Sitting sideways at the little table, his legs neatly crossed, Signor Naccarelli received his coffee, black as pitch. He downed it in one swallow. The general pleasantries about

Florence were duly exchanged. And they were staying? At the Grand. Ah.

"Domani festa," he noted. "I say tomorrow is a holiday, a big one for us here. It is our saint's day, San Giovanni. You have perhaps seen in the Signoria, they are putting up the seats. Do you go?"

Well, she supposed they should really; it was a thing to watch. And the spectacle beforehand? She thought perhaps she could get tickets at the hotel. Signor Naccarelli was struck by an idea. He by chance had extra tickets and the seats were good. She must excuse it if his signora did not come; she was in mourning.

"Oh, I'm very sorry," said Mrs. Johnson.

He waved his hand. No matter. Her family in Naples was a large one; somebody was always dying. He sometimes wore the black band, but then someone might ask him who was dead and if he could not really remember? Che figura! His humor and laugh came and were over as fast as something being broken. "And now—you will come?"

"Well—"

"Good! Then my son will arrange where we are to meet and the hour." He was so quickly on his feet. "Signora." He kissed her hand. "Signorina." Clara had learned to put out her hand quite prettily in the European fashion and she liked to do it. With a nod to Fabrizio, he was gone.

So the next afternoon they were guided expertly through the packed, noisy streets of the festa by Fabrizio, who found them a choice point for watching the parade of the nobles.

It seemed that twice a year, and that by coincidence during the tourist season, Florentine custom demanded that titled gentlemen should wedge themselves into the family suit of armor, mount a horse, and ride in procession, preceded by lesser men in striped knee breeches beating drums. Pennants were twirled as crowds cheered, and while it was doubtless not as thrilling a spectacle as the Palio in Siena, everyone agreed that it was in much better taste. Who in Florence would dream of bringing a horse into church? Afterwards in the piazza, two teams in red and green jerseys would sweat their way through a free-for-all of kicking and running and knocking each other down. This was medieval calcio; the program explained that it was the ancestor of American footballs. Fabrizio, whose English was improving, managed to convey that his brother might have been entitled to ride with the nobles, although it was true he was not in direct line for a title. Instead, his cousin, the Marchese della Valle—there he went now, drooping along on that stupid black horse which was not distinguished. "My brother Giuseppe wish so much to ride today," said Fabrizio. "Also he offer to my cousin the marchese much money." He laughed.

Fabrizio wished his English were equal to relating what a figure Giuseppe had made of himself. The marchese, who was fat, slow-witted and greedy, certainly preferred twenty thousand lire to being pinched black and blue by forty pounds of steel embossed with unicorns. He giggled and said, "Va bene. All right." He sat frankly admiring the tall, swaying lines of Giuseppe's figure and planning what he would do with the money. Giuseppe was carried away by a glorious prevision of himself prancing about the streets amid fluttering pennants, the beat of drums, the gasp of ladies. He swaggered about the room describing his noble bearing astride a horse of such mettle and spirit as would land his cousin the marchese in the street in five minutes, clanging like the gates of hell. He knew where to find it—just such an animal! Nothing like that dull beast that the marchese kept stalled out in the country all year round and that by this time believed himself to be a cow. . . . Unfortunately, the mother of the marchese had been listening all the time behind the door, and took that moment to break in upon them. The whole plan was cancelled in no time at all, and Giuseppe was shown to the door. There was not a drop of nobility in his blood, he was reminded, and no such substitution would be tolerated by the council. As Giuseppe passed down the street, the marchese had flung open the window and called down to him, "Mamma says you only want to impress the American ladies." Everyone in the street had laughed at him and he was furious.

Perhaps it was as well, Fabrizio reflected, not to be able to relate all this to the Signora and Clara. What would they think of his family? It was better not to tell too much. Fabrizio's brother Giuseppe had enjoyed many successes with women and had developed elaborate theories of love which he would discuss in detail, relating examples from his own experience, always with the same serious savor, as if for the first time. No, it was very much wiser not to speak too much of Giuseppe to nice American ladies.

"My father wait for us in the piazza at this moment," Fabrizio said.

Sitting beside Mrs. Johnson in the grandstand during the game, Signor Naccarelli dropped a significant remark or two. Her daughter was charming; his son could think of nothing else. It would be a sad day for Fabrizio when they went away. How nice to think that they would not go away at all, but would spend many months in Florence, perhaps take a small villa. Many outsiders did so. They wished never to leave.

Mrs. Johnson explained her responsibilities at home— her house, her husband and family. And what did Signor Johnson do? A businessman. He owned part interest in a cigarette company and devoted his whole time to the firm. Cigarettes—ah. Signor Naccarelli rattled off all the name brands until he found the right one. Ah.

And her daughter—perhaps the signorina did not wish to leave Florence?

"It is clear that she doesn't," said Mrs. Johnson. And then, she thought, I must tell him now. It was the only sensible thing, and would end this ridiculous dragging on into deeper and deeper complications. She believed that he would understand, even help her to handle things in the right way. "You see—" she began, but just then the small medieval cannon which had fired a blank charge to announce the opening of the contest took a notion to fire again. Nobody ever seemed able to explain why. It was hard to believe that it had ever happened, for in the strong sun the flash of powder, which must have been considerable by another light,

34

had been all but negated. All the players stopped and turned to look, and a man who had been standing between the cannon and the steps of the Palazzo Vecchio fell to the ground. People rushed in around him.

"Excuse me," said Signor Naccarelli. "I think I know him."

There followed a long series of discussions. Signor Naccarelli could be seen waving his hands as he talked. The game went on and everyone seemed to forget the man who every now and then, as the movement around him shifted, could be seen trying to get up. At last, two of the drummers from the parade, still dressed in their knee breeches, edged through the crowd with a stretcher and took him away.

Signor Naccarelli returned as the crowds were dispersing. He had apparently been visiting all the time among his various friends and relatives and appeared to have forgotten the accident. He took off his hat to Mrs. Johnson. "My wife and I invite you to tea with us. On Sunday at four. I have a little car and I will come to your hotel. You will come, no?"

𝒱

TEA AT THE NACCARELLI HOUSEHOLD revealed that the family lived in a spacious apartment with marble floors and had more bad pictures than good furniture. They seemed comfortable, nonetheless, and a little maid in white gloves came and went seriously among them.

The Signora Naccarelli, constructed along ample Neapolitan lines, sat staring first at Clara and then at Mrs. Johnson and smiling at the conversation without understanding a word. Fabrizio sat near her on a little stool, let her pat him occasionally on the shoulder, and gazed tenderly at Clara. Clara sat with her hands folded and smiled at everyone. She had more and more nowadays a rapt air of not listening to anything.

Giuseppe came in, accompanied by his wife. Sealed dungeons doubtless could not have contained them. He said at once in an accent so Middle Western as to be absurd: "How do you do? And how arrre you?" It was all he knew, except Goodbye; he had learned it the day before. Yet he gave the impression that he did not speak out of deference to his father, whose every word he followed attentively, making sure to laugh whenever Mrs. Johnson smiled.

Giuseppe's wife was a slender girl with black hair cut short in the new fashion called simply "Italian." She had French blood, though not as much as she led one to believe. She smoked from a short ivory holder clamped at the side of her mouth, and pretended to regard Giuseppe's amours —of which he had been known to boast in front of her, to the distress of his mama—with a knowing sidelong glance. Sometimes she would remind him of one of his failures. Now she took a place near Fabrizio and chatted with him in a low voice, casting down on him past the cigarette holder the eye of someone old in the ways of love, amused by the eagerness of the young. She looked occasionally at Clara, who beamed at her.

Signor Naccarelli kept the conversation going nicely and seemed to include everybody in the general small talk. There was family anecdote to draw upon; a word or two in Italian sufficed to give the key to which one he was telling now. Some little mention was made of the family villa in a nearby paese, blown up unfortunately by the Allies during the war—the Americans, in fact—but it was indeed a nec- essary military objective and these things happen in all wars. Pazienza. Mrs. Johnson remarked politely on the paintings, but he was quick to admit with a chuckle that they were no good whatsoever. Only one, perhaps; that one over there had been painted by Ghirlandaio—not the famous one in the guide books—on the occasion of some ancestor's wedding, he could not quite remember whose.

"In Florence we have too much history. In America you are so free, free—oh, it is wonderful! Here if we move a stone in the street, who comes? The commission on antiquities, the scholars of the middle ages, priests, professors, committees of everything, saying, 'Do not move it. No, you cannot move it.' And even if you say, 'But it has just this minute fallen on my foot,' they show you no pity. In Rome they are even worse. It reminds me, do you remember the man who fell down when the cannon decide to shoot? Well, he is not well. They say the blood has been poisoned by the infection. If someone had given him penicillin. But nobody did. I hear from my friend who is a doctor at the hospital." He turned to his wife. "No, Mamma? Ti ricordi come ti ho detto. . . ."

When they spoke of the painting, Clara admired it. It was of course a Madonna and Child, all light blue and pink flesh tones. Clara had developed a great all-absorbing interest in these recurring ladies with little baby Jesus on their laps. She had a large collection of dolls at home and had often expressed her wish for a real live little baby brother. She did not see why her mother did not have one. The dolls cried only when she turned them over, they wet their pants only when you pushed something rubber, and so on through eye-closing and walking and saying "Mama." But a real one would do all these things whenever it wanted to. It certainly would, Mrs. Johnson agreed. She was glad those days, at any rate, were over.

Now Clara stared on with parted lips at the painting on which the soft evening light was falling. She had gotten it into her little head recently that Fabrizio and babies were somehow connected. The Signora Naccarelli did not fail to notice the nature of her gaze. On impulse she got up and crossed to sit beside Mrs. Johnson on the couch. She sat facing her and smiling with tears filling her eyes. She was all in black—black stockings, black crepe dress cut in a V at the neck, a small black crucifix on a chain. "Mio figlio," she pronounced slowly, "è buono. Capisce?"

Mrs. Johnson nodded encouragingly. "Si. Capisco."

"Non lui," said the signora, pointing at Giuseppe, who glanced up with a wicked grin—he was delighted to be bad. The signora shook her finger at him. Then she indicated Fabrizio. "Ma lui. Si, è buono. Va in chiesa, capisce?" She put her hands together as if in prayer.

"No, ma Mamma. Che roba!" Fabrizio protested.

"Si, è vero," the signora persisted solemnly; her voice fairly quivered. "È buono. Capisce, signora?"

"Capisco," said Mrs. Johnson.

Everyone complimented her on how well she spoke Italian.

vi

"GALILEO, Dante Alighieri, Boccaccio, Machiavelli, Michelangelo Buonarroti, Donatello, Amerigo Vespucci..." Clara chanted, reading the names off the row of statues of illustrious Tuscans that flanked the street. Her Italian was sounding more clearly every day.

"Hush!" said Mrs. Johnson.

"Leonardo da Vinci, Benvenuto Cellini, Petrarco...." Clara went right on, like a little girl trailing a stick against the palings of a picket fence.

Relations between mother and daughter had deteriorated in recent days. In the full flush of pride at the subjugation of Fabrizio to her every whim, Clara, it is distressing to report, calculated that she could afford to stick out her tongue at her mother, and she did—at times, literally. She refused to pick up her clothes or be on time for any occasion that did not include Fabrizio. She was quarrelsome and she whined about what she didn't want to do, lying with her elbows on the crumpled satin bedspread, staring out of the window. Or she took her parchesi board out of the suitcase and sat cross-legged on the floor with her back to the rugged beauties of the sky line across the Arno, shaking the dice in the wooden cup, throwing for two sets of "men," and tapping out the moves. When called, she did not hear or would not answer; and Mrs. Johnson, smoking nervously in the adjoining room, thought the little sounds would drive her mad. She had never known Clara to show a mean or stubborn side. Yet the minute the girl fell beneath the eye of Fabrizio, her rapt, transported, Madonna look came over her, and she sat still and gentle, docile as a saint, beautiful as an angel. Mrs. Johnson had never beheld such hypocrisy. She had let things go too far, she realized, and whereas before she had been worried, now she was becoming afraid.

Whether she sought advice or whether her need was for somebody to talk things over with, she had gone one day directly after lunch to the American consulate, where she found, on the second floor of a palazzo whose marble halls echoed the click and clack of typing, one of those perpetually young American faces topped by a crew cut. The owner of it was sitting in a seersucker coat behind a standard American office desk in a richly panelled room cut to the noble proportions of the Florentine Renaissance. Memos, docu-

42

ments, and correspondence were arranged in stacks before him, and he looked toward the window while twisting a rubber band repeatedly around his wrist. Mrs. Johnson had no sooner got her first statement out—she was concerned about a courtship between her daughter and a young Italian —than he had cut her off. The consulate could give no advice in personal matters. A priest, perhaps, or a minister or doctor. There was a list of such as spoke English. "Gabriella!" An untidy Italian girl wearing glasses and a green crepe blouse came in from her typewriter in the outer office. "There's a services list in the top of that file cabinet. If you'll just find us a copy." All the while he continued looking out of the window and twisting and snapping the rubber band around his wrist. Mrs. Johnson got the distinct impression that but for this activity he would have dozed right off to sleep. By the time she had descended to the courtyard, her disappointment had turned into resentment. We pay for people like him to come and live in a palace, she thought. It would have helped me just to talk, if he had only listened.

The sun's heat pierced the coarsely woven straw of her little hat and prickled sharply at her tears. The hot street was deserted. Feeling foreign, lonely and exposed, she walked past the barred shops.

The shadowy interior of an espresso bar attracted her. Long aluminum chains in bright colors hung in the door and made a pleasant muted jingling behind her. She sat down at a small table and asked for a coffee. Presently, she opened the mimeographed sheets which the secretary had produced for her. There she found, as she had been told, along with a list of tourist services catering to Americans, rates for exchanging money, and advice on what to do if your passport was lost, the names and addresses of several doctors and members of the clergy. Perhaps it was worth a try. She found a representative of her ancestral faith and noted the obscure address. With her American instinct for getting on with it, no matter what it was, she found her tears and hurt evaporating, drank her coffee and began fumbling through books and maps for the location of the street. She had never dared to use a telephone in Italy.

She went out into the sun. She had left Clara asleep in the hotel during the siesta hour. A lady professor, whose card boasted of a number of university degrees, would come and give Clara an Italian lesson at three. Before this was over, Mrs. Johnson planned to have returned. She motioned to a carrozza and showed the address to the driver, who leaned far back from his seat, almost into her face, to read it. He needed a shave and reeked of garlic and wine. His whip was loud above the thin rump of the horse, and he plunged with a shout into the narrow, echoing streets so gathered-in at this hour as to make any noise seem rude.

After two minutes of this Mrs. Johnson was jerked into a headache. He was going too fast—she had not said she was in a hurry—and taking corners like a madman. "Attenzione!" she called out twice. How did she say *Slow down?* He looked back and laughed at her, not paying the slightest attention to the road ahead. The whip cracked like a pistol shot. The horse slid and, to keep his footing, changed from a trot to a desperate two-part gallop that seemed to be

44

wrenching the shafts from the carriage. Mrs. Johnson closed her eyes and held on. It was probably the driver's idea of a good time. Thank God, the streets were empty. Now the wheels rumbled; they were crossing the river. They entered the quarter of Oltr'arno, the opposite bank, through a small piazza from which a half-dozen little streets branched out. The paving here was of small, rough-edged stones. Speeding toward one tiny slit of a street, the driver, either through mistake or a desire to show off, suddenly wheeled the horse toward another, almost at right angles to them. The beast plunged against the bit that had flung its head and shoulders practically into reverse; and with a great gasp in which its whole lungs seemed involved as in a bellows, it managed to bring its forelegs in line with the new direction. Mrs. Johnson felt her head and neck jerked as cruelly as the horse's had been.

"Stop! STOP!"

At last she had communicated. Crying an order to the horse, hauling in great lengths of rein, the driver obeyed. The carriage stood swaying in the wake of its lost momentum, and Mrs. Johnson alighted shakily in the narrow street. Heads had appeared at various windows above them. A woman came out of a doorway curtained in knotted cords and leaned in the entrance with folded arms. A group of young men, one of them rolling a motorscooter, emerged from a courtyard and stopped to watch.

Mrs. Johnson's impulse was to walk away without a backward glance. She was mindful always, however, of a certain American responsibility. The driver was an idiot, but his family was probably as poor as his horse. She was drawing a five-hundred-lire note from her purse, when, having wrapped the reins to their post in the carrozza, the object of her charity bounded suddenly down before her face. She staggered back, clutching her purse to her. Her wallet had been half out; now his left hand was on it while his right held up two fingers. "Due! Due mila!" he demanded, forcing her back another step. The young men around the motorscooter were noticing everything. The woman in the doorway called a casual word to them and they answered.

"Due mila, signora!" repeated the driver, and thrusting his devil's face into hers, he all but danced.

The shocking thing—the thing that was paralyzing her, making her hand close on the wallet as though it contained something infinitely more precious than twenty or thirty dollars in lire—was the overturn of all her values. He was not ashamed to be seen extorting an unjust sum from a lone woman, a stranger, obviously a lady; he was priding himself rather on showing off how ugly about it he could get. And the others, the onlookers, those average people so depended on by an American to adhere to what is good? She did not deceive herself. Nobody was coming to her aid. Nobody was even going to think, It isn't fair.

She thrust two thousand-lire notes into his hand and, folding her purse closely beneath her arm in ridiculous parody of everything Europeans said about Americans, she hastened away. The driver reared back before his audience. He shook in the air the two notes she had given him. "Mancia! Mancia!" No tip! Turning aside to mount his carriage, he thrust the money into his inner breast pocket, slanting after her a word that makes Anglo-Saxon curses sound like nursery rhymes. She did not understand what it meant, but she felt the meaning; the foul, cold, rat's foot of it ran after her down the street. As soon as she turned a corner, she stopped and stood shuddering against a wall.

Imagine her then, not ten minutes later, sitting on a sofa covered with comfortably faded chintz, steadying her nerves over a cup of tea and talking to a lively old gentleman with a trace of the Scottish highlands in his voice. It had not occurred to her that a Presbyterian minister would be anything but American, but now that she thought of it she supposed that the faith of her fathers was not only Scottish but also French. A memory returned to her, something she had not thought of in years. One Christmas or Thanksgiving as a little girl she had been taken to her grandfather's house in Tennessee. She could reconstruct only a glimpse of something that had happened. She saw herself in the corner of a room with a fire burning and a bay window overlooking an uneven shoulder of side yard partially covered with a light fall of snow. She was meddling with a black book on a little table and an old man with wisps of white hair about his brow was leaning over her: "It's a Bible in Gaelic. Look, I'll show you." And putting on a pair of gold-rimmed glasses he translated strange broken-looking print, moving his horny finger across a tattered page. In this unattractive roughness of things, it was impossible to escape the suggestion of character.

It came to her now in every detail about the man before

her. Even the hairs of his grey brows, thick as wire, had each its own almost contrary notion about where to be, and underneath lived his sharp blue eyes, at once humorous and wry. Far from being disinterested in his unexpected visitor who so obviously had something on her mind, he managed to make Mrs. Johnson feel even more uncomfortable than the specimen of American diplomacy had done. He was, in fact, too interested, alert as a new flame. She had a feeling that compromise was unknown to him, and really, come right down to it, wasn't compromise the thing she kept looking for?

Touching her tea-moistened lip with a small Florentine embroidered handkerchief, she told him her dilemma on quite other terms than the ones that troubled her. She put it to him that her daughter was being wooed by a young Italian of the nicest sort, but naturally a Roman Catholic. This led them along the well-worn paths of theology. The venerable minister, surprisingly, showed little zeal for the workout. An old war horse, he wearied to hurl himself into so trifling a skirmish. He wished to be tolerant . . . his appointment here after retirement had been a joy to him . . . he had come to love Italy, *but*—one could not help observing. . . . For a moment the sparks flew. Well.

Mrs. Johnson took her leave at the door that opened into a narrow dark stair dropping down to the street.

"Ye'll have written to her faither?"

"Why, no," she admitted. His eyelids drooped ever so slightly. Americans . . . divorce; she could see the suspected pattern. "It's a wonderful idea! I'll do it tonight."

48

Her enthusiasm did not flatter him. "If your daughter's religion means anything to her," he said, "I urge ye both to make very careful use of your brains."

Well, thought Mrs. Johnson, walking away down the street, what did Clara's religion mean to her? She had liked to cut out and color things in Sunday school, but she had got too big for that department and no pretense about church-going was kept up any longer. She wanted every year, however, to be an angel in the Christmas pageant. She had been, over the course of the years, every imaginable size of angel. Once, long ago, in a breathless burst of adoration, she had reached into the Winston-Salem First Presbyterian Church Ladies Auxiliary's idea of a manger, a flimsy trough-shaped affair, knocked together out of a Sunkist orange crate, painted gray and stuffed with excelsior. She was looking for the little Lord Jesus, but all she found was a flashlight. Her teacher explained to her, as she stood cheated and tearful, holding this unromantic object in her hands, that it would be sacrilegious to represent the Son of God with a doll. Mrs. Johnson rather sided with Clara; a doll seemed more appropriate than a flashlight.

Now what am I doing? Mrs. Johnson asked herself. Wasn't she employing the old gentleman's warning to reason herself into thinking that Clara's romance was quite all right? More than all right—the very thing? As for writing to Clara's father, why Noel Johnson would be on the trans-Atlantic phone within five minutes after any such suggestion reached him. No, she was alone, really alone.

She sank down on a stone bench in a poor plain piazza

with a rough stone paving, a single fountain, a single tree, a bare church façade, a glare of sun, the sound of some dirty little black-headed waifs playing with a ball. 'Careful use of your brains.' She pressed her hand to her head. Outside the interest of conversation, her headache was returning and the shock of that terrible carriage ride. She did not any longer seem to possess her brains, but to stand apart from them as from everything else in Italy. She had got past the guide books and still she was standing and looking, and her own mind was only one more thing among the things she was looking at, and what was going on in it was like the ringing of so many different bells. Five to four. Oh, my God! She began to hasten away through the labyrinth, the chill stench of the narrow streets.

She must have taken the wrong turning somewhere, because she emerged too far up the river—in fact, just short of the Ponte Vecchio, which she hastened to cross to reach at any rate the more familiar bank. A swirl of tourists hampered her; they were inching along from one show window to the next, of the tiny shops that lined the bridge on both sides, staring at the myriads of baubles, bracelets, watches, and gems displayed there. As she emerged into the street, a handsome policeman, who, dressed in a snow-white uniform, was directing traffic as though it were a symphony orchestra, smiled into the crowd that was approaching along the Lungarno, and brought everything to a dramatic halt.

There, with a nod to him, came Clara! He bowed; she smiled. Why, she looked like an Italian!

Item at a time, mother and daughter had seen things in

the shops they could not resist. Mrs. Johnson with her posi-
tive, clipped American figure found it difficult to wear the
clothes, and had purchased mainly bags, scarves and other
accessories. But Clara could wear almost everything she admired. Stepping along now in her hand-woven Italian skirt
and sleeveless cotton blouse, with leather sandals, smart
straw bag, dark glasses and the glint of earrings against her
cheek, she would fool any tourist into thinking her a native;
and Mrs. Johnson, who felt she was being fooled by Clara
in a far graver way, found in her daughter's very attractive-
ness an added sense of displeasure, almost of disgust.

"Where do you think you're going?" she demanded.

Clara, who was still absorbed in being adored by the
policeman, could not credit her misfortune at having run
into her mother. Mrs. Johnson took her arm and marched
her straight back across the street. Crowds were thronging
against them from every direction. A vender shook a fistful
of cheap leather bags before them; there seemed no escaping
him. Mrs. Johnson veered to the right, entering a quiet street
where there were no shops and where Fabrizio would not
be likely to pass, returning to work after siesta.

"Where were you going, Clara?"

"To get some ice cream," Clara pouted.

"There's ice cream all around the hotel. Now you know
we never tell each other stories, Clara."

"I was looking for you," said Clara.

"But how did you know where I was?" asked Mrs. Johnson.

They had entered the street of the illustrious Tuscans.

"Galileo, Dante Alighieri, Boccaccio, Machiavelli, Michel-angelo . . ." chanted Clara.

This is not my day, sighed Mrs. Johnson to herself.

She was right about this; alighting from her taxi with Clara before the Grand Hotel, she heard a cry behind her:

"Why, Mar-gar-et John-son!"

Two ladies from Winston-Salem stood laughing before her. They were sisters—Meg Kirby and Henrietta Mulver-hill—a chatty, plumpish pair whose husbands had pre-sented them both with a summer abroad.

Now they were terribly excited. They had no idea she would be here still. They had heard she was in Rome by now. What a coincidence! They simply couldn't get over it! Wasn't it wonderful what you could buy here? Linens! Leather-lined bags! So cheap! If only she could see what just this morning—! And how was Clara?

Constrained to go over to the Excelsior—their hotel, just across the street—for tea, Margaret Johnson sat like a creature in a net and felt her strength ebb from her. The handsome salon echoed with Winston-Salem news, gossip, exact quotations, laughter; and during it all, Clara became again her old familiar little lost self, oblivious, searching through her purse, leafing for pictures in the guide books on the tea table, only looking up to say "Yes, ma'am," and "No, ma'am."

"Well, it's just so difficult to pick out a hat for Noel without him here to try it on," said Mrs. Johnson. "I tried it once in Washington, and—" I've been blinded, she thought, the image of her daughter constant in the corner of her vision. Blinded—by what? By beauty, art, strangeness, freedom. By romance, by sun—yes, by hope itself.

By the time she had shaken the ladies, making excuses about dinner but with a promise to call by for them tomorrow, and had reached at long last her hotel room, her headache had grown steadily worse. She yearned to shed her street clothes, take aspirin, and soak in a long bath. Clara passed sulking ahead of her through the anteroom, through the larger bedroom, the bath, and into her own small room. Mrs. Johnson tossed her bag and hat on the bed and, slipping out of her shoes, stepped into a pair of scuffs. A rap at the outer door revealed a servant with a long florist's box. Carrying the box, Mrs. Johnson crossed the bath to her daughter's room.

Through the weeks that they had dallied here, Clara's room had gradually filled with gifts from Fabrizio. A baby elephant of green china, its howdah enlarged to contain brightly wrapped sweets, grinned from a table top. A stuffed dog, Fabrizio's idea of Ronnie, sat near Clara's pillow. On her wrist a charm bracelet was slowly filling with golden miniature animals and tiny musical instruments. She did not have to be told that another gift had arrived, but observed from a glance at the label, as her mother had not, that the flowers were for both of them. Then she filled a tall vase with water. Chores of this sort fell to her at home.

Mrs. Johnson sat down on the bed.

Clara happily read the small card. "It says 'Naccarelli,' " she announced.

Then she began to arrange the flowers in the vase. They

were rather remarkable flowers, Mrs. Johnson thought—a species of lily apparently highly regarded here, though with their enormous naked stamens, based in a back-curling, waxen petal, they had always struck her as being rather blatantly phallic. Observing some in a shop window soon after they had arrived in Florence, it had come to her to wonder then if Italians took sex so much for granted that they hardly thought about it at all, as separate, that is, from anything else in life. Time had passed, and the question, more personal now, still stood unanswered.

The Latin mind—how did it work? What did it think? She did not know, but as Clara stood arranging the flowers one at the time in the vase (there seemed to be a great number of them—far more than a dozen—in the box, and all very large), the bad taste of the choice seemed, in any language, inescapable. The cold eye of Signor Naccarelli had selected this gift, she felt certain, not Fabrizio; and that thought, no less than the flowers themselves, was remarkably effective in short-circuiting romance. Could she be wrong in perceiving a kind of Latin logic at work—its basic quality factual, hard, direct? Even if nobody ever *put* it that way, it was there; and no matter what *she* might think, it was, like the carrozza driver, not in the least ashamed. A demand was closer to being made than she liked to suppose: Exactly where, it seemed to say, did she think all this was leading? She looked at the stuffed dog, at the baby elephant who carried sweets so coyly, at the charm bracelet dancing on Clara's wrist as her hand moved, setting in place one after another the stalks with their sensual bloom.

It's simply that they are facing what I am hiding from, she thought.

"Come here, darling."

She held out her hands to Clara and drew her down on the edge of the bed beside her. Unable to think of anything else to do, she lied wildly.

"Clara, I have just been to the doctor. That is where I went. I didn't tell you—you've been having such a good time—but I'm not feeling well at all. The doctor says the air is very bad for me here and that I must leave. We will come back, of course. As soon as I feel better. I'm going to call for reservations and start packing at once. We will leave for Rome tonight."

Later she nervously penned a note to the ladies at the Excelsior. Clara was not feeling well, she explained, and the doctor had advised their leaving. They would leave their address at American Express in Rome, though there was a chance they might have to go to the Lakes for cooler weather.

vii

TO THE TRAVELLER coming down from Florence to Rome in the summertime, the larger, more ancient city is bound to be a disappointment. It is bunglesome; nothing is orderly or planned; there is a tangle of electric wires and tram lines, a ceaseless clamor of traffic. The distances are long, the sun is hot. And if, in addition, the heart has been left behind as positively as a piece of baggage, the tourist is apt to suffer more than tourists generally do. Mrs. Johnson saw this clearly in her daughter's face. To make things worse, Clara never mentioned Florence or Fabrizio. Mrs. Johnson had only to think of those flowers to keep herself from mentioning either. They had come to see Rome, hadn't they? Very well, Rome would be seen.

At night, after dinner, Mrs. Johnson assembled her guide books and mapped out strenuous tours. Cool cloisters opened before them, and the gleaming halls of the Vatican galleries. They were photographed in the spray of fountains and trailed by pairs of male prostitutes in the park. At Tivoli, Clara had a sunstroke in the ruin of a Roman villa. A goatherd came and helped her to the shade, fanned her with his hat and brought her some water. Mrs. Johnson was afraid for her to drink it. At dusk they walked out the hotel door and saw the whole city in the sunset from the top of the Spanish Steps. Couples stood linked and murmuring together, leaning against the parapets.

"When are we going back, Mother?" Clara asked in the dark.

"Back where?" said Mrs. Johnson, vaguely.

"Back to Florence."

"You want to go back?" said Mrs. Johnson, more vaguely still.

Clara did not reply. To a child, a promise is a promise, a sacred thing, the measure of love. 'We will come back,' her mother had said. She had told Fabrizio so when he came to the station, called unexpectedly out of his shop with this thunderbolt tearing across his heart, clutching a demure mass of wild chrysanthemums and a tin of caramelle. While the train stood open-doored in the station, he had drawn Clara behind a post and kissed her. "We are coming back," said Clara, and threw her arms around him. When he forced down her arms, he was crying, and there stood her mother.

Day by day, Clara followed after Mrs. Johnson's de-

simile

cisive heels, always at the same silent distance, like a good little dog. In the Roman Forum, urged on by the guide book, Mrs. Johnson sought out the ruins of "an ancient basilica containing the earliest known Christian frescoes." They may have been the earliest but to Mrs. Johnson they looked no better than the smeary pictures of Clara's Sunday-school days. She studied them one at a time, consulting her book. When she looked up, Clara was gone. She called once or twice and hastened out into the sun. The ruins before her offered many a convenient hiding place. She ran about in a maze of paths and ancient pavings, until finally, there before her, not really very far away, she saw her daughter sitting on a fallen block of marble with her back turned. She was bent forward and weeping. The angle of her head and shoulders, her gathered limbs, though pained was not pitiful; and arrested by this Mrs. Johnson did not call again, but stood observing how something of a warm, classic dignity had come to this girl, and no matter whether she could do long division or not, she was a woman.

To Mrs. Johnson's credit she waited quietly while Clara straightened herself and dried her eyes. Then the two walked together through the ruin of an open court with a quiet rectangular pool. They went out of the Forum and crossed a busy street to a sidewalk cafe where they both had coffee. In all the crash and clang of the tram lines and the hurry of the crowds there was no chance to speak.

A boy came by, a beggar, scrawny, in clothing deliberately oversized and poor, the trousers held up by a cord, rolled at the cuffs, the bare feet splayed and filthy. A jut of black hair set his swart face in a frame, and the eyes, large, abject, imploring, did not meet now, perhaps had never met, another's. He mumbled some ritualistic phrases and put out a hand that seemed permanently shrivelled into the wrist; the tension, the smear and fear that money was, was in it. In Italy, especially in Rome, Mrs. Johnson had gone through many states of mind about beggars, all the way from Poor things, why doesn't the church do something? to How revolting, why don't they ever let us alone? So she had been known to give them as much as a thousand lire or spurn them like dogs. But something inside her had tired. Clara hardly noticed the child at all; exactly like an Italian, she took a ten-lire piece out of the change on the table and dropped it in his palm. And Mrs. Johnson, in the same way that people crossed themselves with a dabble of holy water in the churches, found herself doing the same thing. He passed on, table by table, and then entered the ceaseless weaving of the crowd, hidden, reappearing, vanishing, lost.

She closed her eyes and, with a sigh that was both qualm and relief, she surrendered.

A lull fell in the traffic. "Clara," she said, "we will go back to Florence tomorrow."

viii

IT WASN'T THAT SIMPLE, of course. Nobody with a dream should come to Italy. No matter how dead and buried the dream is thought to be, in Italy it will rise and walk again. Margaret Johnson had a dream, though she thought reality had long ago destroyed it. The dream was that Clara would one day be perfectly well. It was here that Italy had attacked her, and it was this that her surrender involved.

Then surrender is the wrong word too. Women like Margaret Johnson do not surrender; they simply take up another line of campaign. She would go poised into combat, for she knew already that the person who undertakes to believe in a dream pursues a course that is dangerous and lonely. She knew because she had done it before.

The truth was that when Clara was fourteen and had been removed from school two years previously, Mrs. Johnson had decided to believe that there was not anything the matter with her. It was September, and Noel Johnson was away on a business trip and conference which would last a month. Their son was already away at college. The opportunity was too good to be missed. She chose a school in an entirely new section of town; she told a charming pack of lies and got Clara enrolled there under the most favorable conditions. The next two weeks were probably the happiest of her life. With other mothers, she sat waiting in her car at the curb until the bright crowd came breasting across the campus: Clara's new red tam was the sign to watch for. At night the two of them got supper in the kitchen while Clara told all her stories. Later they did homework, sitting on the sofa under the lamp.

Three teachers came to call at different times. They were puzzled, but were persuaded to be patient. Two days before Noel Johnson was due to come home, Mrs. Johnson was invited to see the principal. Some inquiries, he said, had been felt necessary. He had wished to be understanding, and rather than take the evidence from other reports had done some careful testing of his own under the most favorable circumstances: the child had suspected nothing.

He paused. "I understand that your husband is away." She nodded. "So you have undertaken this—ah—experiment entirely on your own." She nodded again, dumbly. Her throat had tightened. The word "experiment" was damning; she had thought of it herself. No one, of course,

Irony

should experiment with any human being, much less one's own daughter. But wasn't the alternative, to accept things as they were, even worse? It was all too large, too difficult to explain.

The principal stared down at his desk in an embarrassed way. "These realities are often hard for us to face," he said. "Yet, from all I have been able to learn, you did know. It had all been explained to you, along with the best techniques, the limits of her capabilities—"

"Yes," she faltered, "I did know. But I know so much else besides. I know that in so many ways she is as well as you and I. I know that the doctors have said that no final answers have arrived at in these things." She was more confident now. Impressive names could be quoted; statements, if need be, could be found in writing. "Our mental life is not wholly understood as yet. Since no one knows the extent to which a child may be retarded, so no one can say positively that Clara's case is a hopeless one. We know that she is not one bit affected physically. She will continue to grow up just like any other girl. Even if marriage were ever possible to her, the doctors say that her children would be perfectly all right. Everyone sees that she behaves normally most of the time. Do I have to let the few ways she is slow stand in the way of all the others to keep her from being a whole person, from having a whole life—?" She could not go on.

"But those 'few ways,' " he said, consenting, it was obvious, to use her term, "are the main ones we are concerned with here. Don't you see that?"

She agreed. She did see. And yet—

At that same moment, in another part of the building, trivial, painful things were happening to Clara—no one could possibly want to hear about them.

The serene fall afternoon, as she left the school, was as disjointed as if hurricane and earthquake had been at it. Toward nightfall, Mrs. Johnson telephoned to Noel to come home. At the airport, with Clara waiting crumpled like a bundle of clothes on the back seat of the car, she confessed everything to him. When he said little, she realized he thought she had gone out of her mind. Clara was sent to the country to visit an aunt and uncle, and Mrs. Johnson spent a month in Bermuda. Strolling around the picture-postcard landscape of the resort, she said to herself, I was out of my mind, insane. As impersonal as advertising slogans, or skywriting, the words seemed to move out from her, into the golden air.

Courage, she thought now, in a still more foreign landscape, riding the train back to Florence. Coraggio. The Italian word came easily to mind. Mrs. Johnson belonged to various clubs, and campaigns to clean up this or raise the standards of that were frequently turned over to committees headed by her. She believed that women in their way could accomplish a great deal. What was the best way to handle Noel? How much did the Naccarellis know? As the train drew into the station, she felt her blood race, her whole being straighten and poise, to the fine alertness of a drawn bow. Whether Florence knew it or not, she invaded it.

As for how much the Naccarelli family knew or didn't know or cared or didn't care, no one not Italian had better undertake to say. It was never clear. Fabrizio threatened suicide when Clara left. The mother of Clara had scorned him because he was Italian. No other reason. Everyone had something to say. The household reeled until nightfall when Fabrizio plunged toward the central open window of the salotto. The serious little maid, who had been in love with him for years, leaped in front of him with a shriek, her arms thrown wide. Deflected, he rushed out of the house and went tearing away through the streets. The Signora Naccarelli collapsed in tears and refused to eat. She retired to her room, where she kept a holy image that she placed a great store by. Signor Naccarelli alone enjoyed his meal. He said that Fabrizio would not commit suicide and that the ladies would probably be back. He had seen Americans take fright before; no one could ever explain why. But in the end, like everyone else, they would serve their own best interests. If he did not have some quiet, he would certainly go out and seek it elsewhere.

He spent the pleasantest sort of afternoon locked in conversation with Mrs. Johnson a few days after her return. It was all an affair for juggling, circling, balancing, very much to his liking. He could not really say she had made a conquest of him: American women were too confident and brisk; but he could not deny that encounters with her had a certain flavor.

The lady had consented to go with him on a drive up to San Miniato, stopping at the casino for a cup of tea and a pastry. Signor Naccarelli managed to get in a drive to Bello Sguardo as well, and many a remark about young love and many a glance at his companion's attractive legs and figure. Margaret Johnson achieved a cool but not unfriendly position while folding herself into and out of a car no bigger than an enclosed motorcycle. The management of her skirt alone was enough to occupy her entire attention.

"They are in the time of life," Signor Naccarelli said, darting the car through a narrow space between two motorscooters, "when each touch, each look, each sigh arises from the heart, the heart alone." He removed his hands from the wheel to do his idea homage, flung back his head and closed his eyes. Then he snapped to and shifted gears. "For them love is without thought, as to draw breath, to sleep, to walk. You and I—we have come to another stage. We have known all this before—we think of the hour, of some business—so we lose our purity, who knows how? It is sad, but there is nothing to do. But we can see our children. I do not say for Fabrizio, of course—it would be hard to find a young Florentine who has had no experience. I myself at a younger age, at a much younger age—do you know my first love was a peasant girl? It was at the villa where I had gone out with my father. A contadina. The spring was far along. My father stayed too long with the animals. I became, how shall I say?—bored, yes, but something more also. She was very beautiful. I still can dream of her, only her—I never succeed to dream of others. I do not know if your daughter will be for Fabrizio the first, or will not be. I would say not, but still—he is figlio di mamma, a

66

good boy —I do not know." He frowned. They turned suddenly and shot up a hill. When they gained the crest, he came to a dead stop and turned to Mrs. Johnson. "But for her he has the feeling of the first woman! I am Italian and I tell you this. It is unmistakable! That, cara signora, is what I mean to say." Starting forward again, the car wound narrowly between tawny walls richly draped with vines. They emerged on a view, and stopped again. Cypress, river, hill, and city like a natural growth among them—they looked down on Tuscany. The air was fresher here but undoubtedly very hot below. There was a slight haze, just enough to tone away the glare; but even on the distant blue hills outlines of a tree or a tower were distinct to the last degree—one had the sense of being able to see everything exactly as it was.

"There is no question with Clara," Mrs. Johnson murmured. "She has been very carefully brought up."

"Not like other American girls, eh? In Italy we hear strange things. Not only hear. Cara signora, we *see* strange things also. You can imagine. Never mind. The signorina is another thing entirely. My wife has noticed it at once. Her innocence." His eye kept returning to Mrs. Johnson's knee, which in the narrow silk skirt of her dress it was difficult not to expose. Her legs were crossed and her stocking whitened the flesh.

"She is very innocent," said Mrs. Johnson.

"And her father? How does he feel? An Italian for his daughter? Well, perhaps in America you, too, hear some strange words about us. We are no different from others, except we are more—well, you see me here—we are here together—it is not unpleasant—I look to you like any other man. And yet perhaps I feel a greater—how shall I say? You will think I play the Italian when I say there is a greater—"

She did think just that. She had been seriously informed on several occasions recently that Anglo-Saxons knew very little about passion, and now Signor Naccarelli, for whom she had a real liking, was about to work up to the same idea. She pulled down her skirt with a jerk. "There are plenty of American men who appreciate women just as much as you do," she told him.

He burst out laughing. "Of course! We make such a lot of foolishness, signora. But on such an afternoon—" His gesture took in the landscape. "I spoke of your husband. I think to myself, He is in cigarettes, after all. A very American thing. When you get off the boat, what do you say? 'Where is Clara?' says Signor Johnson. 'Where is my leetle girl?' 'Clara, ah!' you say. 'She is back in Italy. She has married with an Italian. I forgot to write you—I was so busy.'"

"But I write to him constantly!" cried Mrs. Johnson. "He knows everything. I have told him about you, about Fabrizio, the signora, Florence, all these things."

"But first of all you have considered your daughter's heart. For yourself, you could have left us, gone, gone. Forever. Not even a postcard." He chuckled. Suddenly he took a notion to start the car. It backed at once, as if a child had it on a string, then leaping forward fairly toppled over the crest of a steep run of hill down into the city, speeding as fast as a roller skate. Mrs. Johnson clutched her hat. "When my son was married," she cried, "my husband wrote out a check for five thousand dollars. I have reason to think he will do the same for Clara."

"Ma che generoso!" cried Signor Naccarelli, and it seemed he had hardly said it before he was jerking the hand brake to prevent their entering the hotel lobby.

She asked him in for an apéritif. He leaned flirtatiously at her over a small round marble-topped table. The plush decor of the Grand Hotel, with its gilt and scroll-edged mirrors that gave back wavy reflections, reminded Mrs. Johnson of middle-aged adultery, one party only being titled. But neither she nor Signor Naccarelli was titled. It was a relief to know that sin was not expected of them. If she were thinking along such lines, heaven only knew what was running in Signor Naccarelli's head. Almost giggling, he drank down a red, bitter potion from a fluted glass.

"So you ran away," he said, "upset; you could not bear the thought. You think and you think. You see the signorina's unhappy face. You could not bear her tears. You return. It is wise. There should be a time for thought. This I have said to my wife, to my son. But when you come back, they say to me, 'But if she leaves again—?' But I say, 'The signora is a woman who is without caprice. She will not leave again.' "

"I do not intend to leave again," said Mrs. Johnson, "until Clara and Fabrizio are married."

As if on signal, at the mention of his name, Fabrizio himself stepped before her eyes, but at some distance away, outside the archway of the salon, which he had evidently had the intention of entering if something had not distracted him. His moment of distraction itself was pure grace, as if a creature in nature, gentle to one word only, had heard that word. There was no need to see that Clara was somewhere within his gaze.

Signor Naccarelli and Mrs. Johnson rose and approached the door. They were soon able to see Clara above stairs—she had promised to go no farther—leaning over, her hair falling softly past her happy face. "Ciao," she said finally, "come stai?"

"Bene. E tu?"

"Bene."

Fabrizio stood looking up at her for so long a moment that Mrs. Johnson's heart had time almost to break. Gilt, wavy mirrors, and plush decor seemed washed clean, and all the wrong, hurt years of her daughter's affliction were not proof against the miracle she saw now.

Fabrizio was made aware of the two in the doorway. He had seen his father's car and stopped by. A cousin kept his shop for him almost constantly nowadays. It was such a little shop, while he—he wished to be everywhere at once. Signor Naccarelli turned back to Mrs. Johnson before he followed his son from the lobby. There were tears in her eyes; she thought perhaps she observed something of the same in his own. At any rate, he was moved. He grasped her hand tightly, and his kiss upon it as he left her said to her more plainly than words, she believed, that they had shared together a beautiful and touching moment.

ix

LETTERS, INDEED, had been flying; the air above the Atlantic was thick with them. Margaret Johnson sat up nights over them. A shawl drawn round her, she worked at her desk near the window overlooking the Arno, her low night light glowing on the tablet of thin airmail stationery. High diplomacy in the olden days perhaps proceeded thus, through long cramped hours of weighing one word against another, striving for just the measure of language that would sway, persuade, convince.

She did not underestimate her task. In a forest of question marks, the largest one was her husband. With painstaking care, she tried to consider everything in choosing her tone: Noel's humor, the season, their distance apart, how busy he was, how loudly she would have to speak to be heard.

Frankly, she recalled the time she had forced Clara into school; she admitted her grave error. Point at a time, she contrasted that disastrous sequence with Clara's present happiness. One had been a plan, deliberately contrived, she made clear; whereas, here in Florence, events had happened of their own accord.

"The thing that impresses me most, Noel (she wrote), is that nothing beyond Clara ever seems to be required of her here. I do wonder if anything beyond her would ever be required of her. Young married girls her age, with one or two children, always seem to have a nurse for them; a maid does all the cooking. There are mothers and mothers-in-law competing to keep the little ones at odd hours. I doubt if these young wives ever plan a single meal.

"Clara is able to pass every day here, as she does at home, doing simple things which please her. But the difference is that here, instead of being always alone or with the family, she has all of Florence for company and seems no different from the rest. Every afternoon she dresses in her pretty clothes and we walk to an outdoor cafe to meet with some young friends of the Naccarellis. You would be amazed how like them she has become. She looks more Italian every day. They prattle. About what? Well, as far as I can follow—Clara's Italian is so much better than mine—about movie stars, pet dogs, some kind of car called

Alfa-Romeo, and what man is handsomer than what other man.

"I understand that usually in the summer all these people go to the sea, where they spend every day for a month or two swimming and lying in the sun. They would all be there now if Fabrizio's courtship had not so greatly engaged their interest. Courtship is the only word for it. If you could see how he adores Clara and how often he mentions the very same things that we love in her: her gentleness, her sweetness and goodness. I had expected things to come to some conclusion long before now, but nothing of the sort seems to occur, and now the thought of separating the two of them begins to seem more and more wrong to me, every day. . . ."

This letter provoked a trans-Atlantic phone call. Mrs. Johnson went to the lobby to talk, so Clara wouldn't hear her. She knew what the first words would be. To Noel Johnson, the world was made of brass tacks, and coming down to them was his specialty.

"Margaret, are you thinking that Clara should marry this boy?"

"I'm only trying to let things take their natural course."

"*Natural* course!" Even at such a distance, he could make her jump.

"I'm with her constantly, Noel. I don't mean they're left to themselves. I only mean to say I can't wrench her away from him now. I tried it. Honestly I did. It was too much for her. I saw that."

"But surely you've talked to these people, Margaret.

You must have told them all about her. Don't any of them speak English?" It would seem unbelievable to Noel Johnson that she or anyone related to him in any way would have learned to communicate in any language but English. He would be sure they had got everything wrong.

"I've tried to explain everything fully," she assured him. Well, hadn't she? Was it her fault a cannon had gone off just when she meant to explain?

Across the thousands of miles she heard his breath and read its quality: he had hesitated. Her heart gave a leap.

"Would I encourage anything that would put an ocean between Clara and me?"

She had scored again. Mrs. Johnson's deepest rebellion against her husband had occurred when he had wanted to put Clara in a sort of "school" for "people like her." The rift between them on that occasion had been a serious one, and though it was smoothed over in time and never mentioned subsequently, Noel Johnson might still not be averse to putting distances between himself and his daughter.

"They're just after her money, Margaret."

"No, Noel—I wrote you about that. They *have* money." She shut her eyes tightly. "And nobody wants to come to America, either."

When she put down the phone a few minutes later, Mrs. Johnson had won a concession. Things should proceed along their natural course, very well. But she was to make no permanent decision until Noel himself could be with her. His coming, at the moment, was next to impossible. Business was pressing. One of the entertainers employed to

74

advertise the world's finest smoke on a national network had been called up by the Un-American Activities Committee. The finest brains in the company were being exercised far into the night. It would not do for the American public to conclude they were inhaling Communism with every puff on a well-known brand. This could happen; it could ruin them. Noel would go to Washington in the coming week. It would be three weeks at least until he could be with her. Then—well, she could leave the decision up to him. If it involved bringing Clara home with them, he would take the responsibility of it on himself.

Noel and Margaret Johnson gravely wished each other good luck over the trans-Atlantic wire, and each resumed the burden of his separate enterprise.

Angry tone

"Where'd you go, Mother?" Clara wanted to know, as soon as Mrs. Johnson returned.

"You'll never guess. I've been talking with Daddy on the long-distance phone!"

"Oh!" Clara looked up. She had been sitting on a footstool shoved back against the wall of her mother's room, writing in her diary. "Why didn't you tell me?"

"I didn't know that's who it was," she lied.

"But I wanted to talk to him, too!"

"What would you have said?"

"I would have said—" She hesitated, thinking hard, staring past her mother into the opposite wall, her young brow contracting faintly. "I would have said: 'Ciao. Come stai?'"

"Would Daddy have understood?"

"I would have told him," Clara said faithfully.

After that she said nothing more but leaned her head against the wall, and forgetful of father, mother, and diary, she stared before her with parted lips, dreaming.

Oh, my God, Margaret Johnson thought. How glad I am that Noel is coming to get me out of this!

x

AFTER HER HUSBAND's telephone call, Margaret Johnson
went to bed in as dutiful and obedient a frame of mind as
any husband of whatever nationality could wish for. She
awoke flaming with new anxiety, confronted by the simplest
truth in the world.

If Noel Johnson came to Florence, he would spoil everything. She must have known that all along.

He might not mean to—she gave him the benefit of the
doubt. But he would do it. Given a good three days, her
dream would all lie in little bright bits on the floor, like
the remains of the biggest and most beautiful Christmas
tree ornament in the world.

For one thing, there was nothing in the entire Florentine day that would not seem especially designed to irritate Noel Johnson. From the coffee he would be asked to drink in the morning, right through the siesta, when every shop, including his prospective son-in-law's, shut up at the very hour when they could be making the most money; up through midnight when mothers were still abroad with their babies in the garrulous streets—he would have no time whatsoever for this inefficient way of life. Was there any possible formation of stone and paint hereabout that would not remind him uncomfortably of the Catholic Church? In what frame of mind would he be cast by Fabrizio's cuffless trousers, little pointed shoes, and carefully dressed hair? No, three days was a generous estimate; he would send everything sky-high long before that. And though he might regret it, he would never be able to see what he had done that was wrong.

His wife understood him. She sat over her caffé latte at her by-now-beloved window above the Arno, and while she thought of him a peculiarly tender and generous smile played about her face. "Clara," she called gently, "have you written to Daddy recently?" Clara was splashing happily in the bathtub and did not hear her.

Soon Mrs. Johnson rose to get her cigarettes from the dresser, but stopped in the center of the room, where she stood with her hand to her brow for a long time, so enclosed in thought she could not have told where she was.

If she went back on her promise to Noel to do nothing until he came, the whole responsibility of action would be her own, and in the very moment of taking it, she would have to begin to lie. To lie in Winston-Salem was one thing, but to start lying to everybody in Italy—why, Italians were past masters at this sort of thing. Wouldn't they see through her at once? Perhaps they already had.

She could never quite get it out of her mind that perhaps, indeed, they already had. Her heart had occasionally quite melted to the idea—especially after a glass of wine—that the Italian nature was so warm, so immediate, so intensely personal, that they had all perceived at once that Clara was a child and had loved her anyway, for what she was. They had not, after all, gone the dreary round from doctor to doctor, expert to expert, in the dwindling hope of finding some way to make the girl "normal." They did not *think,* after all, in terms of IQ, "retarded mentality" and "adult capabilities." And why, oh, why, Mrs. Johnson had often thought, since she too loved Clara for herself, should any-one think of another human being in the light of a set of terms?

But though she might warm to the thought—and since she never learned the answer she never wholly discarded it—she always came to the conclusion that she could not act upon it, and had to put it aside as being, for all practical purposes, useless. "Ridiculous," she could almost hear Noel Johnson say. Mrs. Johnson came as near as she ever had in her life to wringing her hands. Oh, my God, she thought, if he comes here!

But she did not, that morning, seek out advice from any crew-cut diplomat or frosty-eyed Scot. At times she came flatly to the conclusion that she would stick to her promise to Noel because it was right to do so (she believed in doing right), and that since it was right, no harm could come of it. At other times, she wished she could believe this.

In the afternoon, she accompanied Clara to keep an appointment at a cafe with Giuseppe's wife Franca and another girl. She left the three of them enjoying pretty pastries and chattering happily of movie stars, dogs, and the merits of the Alfa-Romeo. Clara had learned so much Italian that Mrs. Johnson could no longer understand her.

Walking distractedly, back of the hotel, away from the river, she soon left the tourist-ridden areas behind her. She went thinking, unmindful of the people who looked up with curiosity as she passed. Her thought all had one center: her husband.

Never before had it seemed so crucial that she see him clearly. What was the truth about him? It had to be noted first of all, she believed, that Noel Johnson was in his own and everybody else's opinion a good man. Meaning exactly what? Well, that he believed in his own goodness and the goodness of other people, and would have said, if asked, that there must be good people in Italy, Germany, Tasmania, even Russia. On these grounds he would reason correctly that the Naccarelli family might possibly be as nice as his wife said they were.

Still, he did not think—fundamentally, he doubted, and Margaret had often heard him express something of the sort—that Europeans really had as much sense as Americans. Intellect, education, art, and all that sort of thing—

well, maybe. But ordinary sense? Certainly, he was in grave doubts here when it came to the Latin races. And come right down to it (in her thoughts she slipped easily into Noel's familar phrasing), didn't his poor afflicted child have about as much sense already as any Italian? His first reaction would have been to answer right away: Probably she does. Other resentments sprang easily to his mind when touched on this sensitive point. Americans had had to fight two awful wars to get Europeans out of their infernal messes. He had a right to some sensitivity, anyone must admit. In the first war he had risked his life; his son had been wounded in the second; and if that were not enough he could always remember his income tax. But there was no use getting really worked up. Some humor would prevail here, and he was not really going to lose sleep over something he couldn't help.

But Clara, now (she could almost hear him saying), this thing of Clara. There Margaret Johnson could grieve for Noel, almost more than for herself. Something had happened here which he was powerless to do anything about; a chance accident had turned into a persisting and delicate matter, affecting his own pretty little daughter in this final way. An ugly finality, and no decent way of disposing of it. A fact he had to live with, day after day. An abnormality; hence, to a man like himself, a source of horror. For wasn't he dedicated, in his very nature, to "doing something about" whatever was not right?

How, she wondered, had Noel spent yesterday afternoon, after he had replaced the telephone in his study at home? She could tell almost to a T, no crystal-ball gazing required. He would have wandered, thinking, about the rooms for a time, unable to put his mind on the next morning's committee meeting. As important as it was that no Communist crooner should leave a pink smear on so American an outfit as their tobacco company, he would not have been able to concentrate. He likely would have entered the living room only to find Clara's dog Ronnie lying under the piano, a spot he favored during the hot months. They would have looked at one another, the two of them, disputing something. Then he would presently have found himself before the icebox, making a ham sandwich perhaps, snapping the cap from a cold bottle of beer. Tilting beer into his mouth with one hand, eating with the other, he might later appear strolling about the yard. It might occur to him (she hoped it had) that he needed to speak to the yard man about watering the grass twice a week so it wouldn't look like the Sahara desert when they returned. When *they* returned! With Clara, or without her? Qualms swept her. Her heart went down like an elevator.

"Signora! Attenzione!"

The voice was from above. A window had been pushed wide and a woman was leaning out to shake a carpet into the street. Margaret Johnson stopped, stepping back a few paces. Dust flew down, then settled. An arm came out and closed the shutters. She went on.

And quite possibly Noel, then, as dusk fell, his mind being still unsettled, would have walked over three blocks and across the park to his sister Isabel's apartment. Didn't he, in personal matters, always turn to women? Isabel, yes, would be the first to hear the news from abroad. She would not be as satisfactory a listener as Margaret, for being both a divorcee and something of a businesswoman (she ran the hat department in Winston-Salem's largest department store) she was inclined to be entirely too casual about everybody's affairs except her own. She would be beautifully dressed in one of her elaborate lounging outfits, for nobody appreciates a Sunday evening at home quite so much as a working woman. She would turn off the television to accommodate Noel, and bring him a drink of the very best Scotch. When she had heard the entire story of the goings-on in Florence, she would as likely as not say, "Well, after all, why not?" Hadn't she always advanced the theory that Clara had as much sense as most of the women she sold hats to? "They're going to want a dowry," she might add.

Now, mentioning a dowry that way would be all to the good. Noel would feel a great relief. He disliked being taken advantage of, and he was obviously uneasy that the Naccarellis were only after Clara's money. Wouldn't Margaret be staying in the best hotel, eating at the best restaurants, shopping in the best shops? The Italians had "caught on," of course, from the first, that she was well off. But now, through Isabel, he would have a name for all this. Dowry. It was customary. "Of course, they're all Catholics," he would go on to complain. Isabel would not be of any use at all there. Religion was of no interest to her whatever. She could not see why it was of interest to anybody.

Later, as they talked, Isabel would ask Noel about the

communist scare. She would be in doubt that the crooner was actually such a threat to the nation or the tobacco company that a song or two would ruin them all; and was all this trouble and upset necessary—trips to Washington, committee meetings, announcements of policy and what not? Noel would not be above reminding her that she liked her dividend checks well enough not to want them put in any jeopardy. He might not come right out and say this, but it would cross his mind. More and more in recent years, Noel's every experience found immediate reference in his business. Or had he always been this way, if, in his younger years, less obviously so? Yet Mrs. Johnson remembered once on a summer vacation they had taken at Myrtle Beach during the depression, Noel playing ball on the sand with the two children when a wind had driven them inside their cottage and for a short time they had been afraid a hurricane was starting. How they had saved to make that trip!— that was all Noel could recall about it in later years. But at the time he had remarked as the raw wind streamed sand against the thin tremulous walls—he was holding Clara in his lap—"Well, at least we're all together." The wind had soon dropped, and the sea had enjoyed a quiet green dusk; their fear had gone, too, but she could not forget the steadying effect of his words. When, at what subtle point, had money come to seem to him the very walls that kept out the storm? Or was the trouble simply that with Clara and her problem always before him at home, he had found business to be a thing he could, at least, handle successfully, as he could not, in common with all mankind (poor Noel!), ulti-

mately "handle" life? And business was, after all, so
"normal."

Whatever the answer to how it had happened—and perhaps the nature of the times had had a lot to do with it:
depression, the New Deal, the war—the fact was that it had
happened, and Margaret knew now that nothing on earth
short of the news of the imminent death of herself or Clara,
or both, could induce Noel Johnson to Florence until the
business in hand was concluded to the entire satisfaction of
the tobacco company, whose future must, at all personal
cost, be secure. On the other hand, since she had already
foreseen that if he came here he would spoil everything,
wasn't this an advantage?

She had wandered, in this remote corner of the city, into
a small, poor bar. She lighted a cigarette and asked for a
coffee. Since there was no place to sit, she stood at the
counter. Two young men were working back of the bar, and
seeing that she only stared at her coffee without drinking
it, they became extremely anxious to make her happy. They
wondered whether the coffee was hot enough, if she wanted
more sugar or some other thing perhaps. She shook her
head, smiling her thanks, seeing as though from a distance
their great dim eyes, their white teeth, and their kindness.
"Simpatica," one said, more about her than to her. "Si,
simpatica," the other agreed. They exchanged a nod. One
had an inspiration. "Americana?" he asked.

"Si," said Mrs. Johnson.

They stood back, continuing to smile like adults who
watch a child, while she drank her coffee down. At this

moment, she had the feeling that if she had requested their giant espresso machine, which seemed, besides a few cheap cups and saucers and a pastry stand, to be their only possession, they would have ripped it up bodily and given it to her. And perhaps, for a moment, this was true.

What is it, to reach a decision? It is like walking down a long Florentine street where, at the very end, a dim shape is waiting until you get there. When Mrs. Johnson finally reached this street and saw what was ahead, she moved steadily forward to see it at long last up close. What was it? Well, nothing monstrous, it seemed; but human, with a face much like her own, that of a woman who loved her daughter and longed for her happiness.

"I'm going to do it," she thought. "Without Noel."

xi

SIGNOR NACCARELLI was late coming home for lunch the next day; the water in the pasta pot had boiled away once and had to be replenished. He was not as late, however, as he had been many times before, or as late as he would have preferred to be that day; and though his news was good, his temper was short. Signora Johnson had talked with her husband on the telephone from America. Signor Johnson could not come to Italy from America. He could not leave his business. They were to proceed with the wedding without Signor Johnson. He neatly baled mouthfuls of spaghetti on his fork, mixed mineral water with a little wine, and found ways of cutting off the effusive rejoicing his family was given to. The real fact was that he was displeased with the American signora. Why, after dressing herself in the new Italian costume of printed white silk which must have cost at least 60,000 lire in the Via Tournabuoni—and with the chic little hat, too—should she give him her news and then leave him in the cafe after thirty minutes, saying "lunch" and "time to go" and "Clara"? American women were at the mercy of their children. It was shocking and disgusting. She had made the appointment with him, well and good. In the most fashionable cafe in Florence, they had been observed talking deeply together over an apéritif in the shadow of a great green umbrella. It would not be the first time he had been observed with this lady about the city. And then, after thirty minutes—! An Italian man would see to manners of this sort. This bread was stale. Were they all eating it, or was it saved from last week, especially for him?

Signora Naccarelli, meanwhile, from the mention of the word "wedding," had quietly taken over everything. She had been more or less waiting up to this time, neither impatient nor anxious, but, like a natural force, quite aware of how inevitable she was, while the others debated and decided superficial affairs. The heart of the matter in Signora Naccarelli's view was so overwhelmingly enormous that she did not have to decide to heed it, because there was nothing outside of it to make this decision. She simply *was* the heart—that great pulsing organ which could bleed with sorrow, or make little fish-like leaps of joy, and which always knew just what it knew. What it knew in Signora Naccarelli's case was very little and quite sufficient. Her son, Fabrizio, was handsome and good, and Clara, the little American flower, so sweet and gentle, would bear children for him. The signora's arms had yearned for some time for Clara and were already beginning to yearn for her children, and this to the signora was exactly the same thing as saying that the arms of the Blessed Virgin yearned for Clara and for Clara's children, and this in turn was the same as saying that the Holy Mother Church yearned likewise. It was all very simple and true.

Informed with such certainties, Signora Naccarelli had not been inactive. A brother of a friend of her nephew was a priest who had studied in England. She had fixed on him already, since he spoke English, as the very one for Clara's instruction. That same afternoon she set about arranging a time for them to meet. Within a few days, the priest was reporting to her that Clara had a real devotion to the Virgin. The signora had known all along that this was true. A distant cousin of Signor Naccarelli's was secretary to a Monsignore at the Vatican, and through him special permission was obtained for Clara to be married in a full church ceremony. At this the signora's joy could not be contained, and she went so far as to telephone Mrs. Johnson and explain these developments to her, a word at the time, in Italian, at the top of her voice, with tears.

"Capisce, signora? In chiesa! Capisce?"

Mrs. Johnson did not capisce. She thought from the tears that something must have gone wrong.

But nothing had, or did, until the morning in the office of the parroco, where they gathered a little more than two weeks before the wedding to fill out the appropriate forms.

xii

WHAT HAD HAPPENED was not at all clear for some time; it
was not even clear that anything had.

The four of them—Clara and Fabrizio, with Margaret
Johnson and Signor Naccarelli for witnesses—were assembled in the office of the parroco, a small dusty room with a
desk, a few chairs and several locked cabinets that reached
to the ceiling, and one window looking down on a cloister.
In the center of the cloister was a hexagonal medieval well.
It was nearing noon. Whatever noise there was seemed to
gather itself together and drowse in the sun on the stone
pavings below, so that Mrs. Johnson experienced the re-
assuring tranquility of silence. Signor Naccarelli, hat in

hand, took a nervous turn or two around the office, looked at a painting that was propped in the back corner, and with a sour down-turning of his mouth said something uncomplimentary about priests which Mrs. Johnson did not quite catch. Fabrizio sat by Clara and twirled a clever straw ornament attached to her bag. So much stone was all that kept them cool. The chanting in the church below had stopped, but the priest did not come.

The hours ahead were planned: they would go to lunch to join Giuseppe and Franca his wife and two or three other friends. Of course, Mrs. Johnson was explaining to herself, this smell of candle smoke, stone dust, and oil painting is to them just what blackboards, chalk and old Sunday-school literature are to us; there's probably no difference at all if you stay open-minded. To be ready for the questions that they were there to answer, she made sure that she had brought her passport and Clara's. She drew them out of their appropriate pocket in the enormous bag Winston-Salem's best department store had advised for European travel, and held them ready.

Signor Naccarelli decided to amuse her. He sat down beside her. Documents, he explained in a jaunty tone, were the curse of Italy. You could not become a corpse in Italy without having filled in the proper document. There were people in offices in Rome still sorting documents filed there before the war. What war? they would say if you told them. But, Mrs. Johnson assured him, all this kind of thing went on in America too. The files were more expensive perhaps. She got him to laugh. His quick hands picked up the passports. Clara and Fabrizio were whispering to one another. Their voices too seemed to go out into the sun, like a neighborhood sound. Signor Naccarelli glanced at Mrs. Johnson's passport picture—how terrible! She was much more beautiful than this. Clara's next—this of the signorina was better, somewhat. A page turned beneath his thumb.

A moment later, Signor Naccarelli had leaped up as though stung by a bee. He hastened to Fabrizio, to whom he spoke rapidly in Italian; then he shot from the room. Fabrizio leaped up also. "Ma Papà! Non possiamo fare nulla—!" The priest came, but it was too late. He and Fabrizio entered into a long conversation. Clara retreated to her mother's side. When Fabrizio turned to them at last, he seemed to have forgotten all his English. "My father—forget—remember—the appointments," he blundered. Struck by an idea, he whirled back to the priest and embarked on a second conversation which he finally summarized to Clara and her mother: "Tomorrow."

At that, precisely as though he were a casual friend who hoped to see them again sometime, he bowed over Mrs. Johnson's hand, made an appropriate motion to Clara, and turned away. They were left alone with the priest.

"Tomorrow" . . . "domani" Mrs. Johnson knew by now to be the word in Italy most likely to signal the finish of everything. She felt, indeed, without the ghost of an idea how or why it had happened, that everything was trembling, tottering about her, had perhaps, without her knowledge, already collapsed. She looked out on the priest like someone seen across a gulf. As if to underscore the impression, he spread his hands with a little helpless shrug and said, "No Eeenglish."

Mrs. Johnson zipped the passports back into place and went out into the corridor, down the steps and into the sun. "Domani," the priest said after them.

Holding Clara by the hand, she made her way back to the hotel.

The instant she was alone she had the passports out, searching through them. Would nothing give her a clue to what had struck Signor Naccarelli? She remembered stories: the purloined letter; the perfect crime, marred only by the murderer's driver's license left carelessly on the hotel dresser. What had she missed? She thought her nerves would fly apart in all directions.

Slowly, with poise and majesty, the beautiful afternoon went by. A black cloud crossed the city, flashed two or three fierce bolts, rumbled half-heartedly and passed on. The river glinted under the sun, and the boys and fishermen who had not been frightened inside shouted and laughed at the ones who had. Everything stood strongly exposed in sunlight and cast its appropriate shadow: in Italy there is the sense that everything is clear and visible, that nothing is withheld. Fabrizio, when Margaret Johnson had touched his arm to detain him in the office of the parroco, had drawn back like recoiling steel. When Clara had started forward with a cry, he had set her quickly back, and silent. If they were to be rejected, had they not at least the right to common courtesy? What were they being given to understand? In Florence, at four o'clock, everything seemed to take a step nearer, more distinctly, more totally to be seen.

When the cloud came up, Mrs. Johnson and Clara clung together pretending that was what they were afraid of. Later they got out one of Clara's favorite books: Nancy Drew, the lady detective, turned airline hostess to solve the murder of a famous explorer. Nancy Drew had so far been neglected. Clara was good and did as she was told about everything, but could not eat. Late in the evening, around ten, the telephone rang in their suite. A gentleman was waiting below for the signora.

Coming down alone, Mrs. Johnson found Signor Naccarelli awaiting her, but how changed! If pleasant things had passed between them, he was not thinking of them now; one doubted that they had actually occurred. Grave, gestureless, as though wrapped in a black cape, he inclined to her deeply. Margaret Johnson had trouble keeping herself from giggling. Wasn't it all a comedy? If somebody would only laugh out loud with enough conviction, wouldn't it all crumble? But she recalled Clara, her eye feasting on Fabrizio's shoulder, her finger exploring the inspired juncture of his neck and spine; and so she composed herself and allowed herself to be escorted from the hotel.

She saw at once that his object was to talk and that he had no destination—they walked along the river. The heat had been terrible for a week, but a breeze was blowing off the water now and she wished she had brought her shawl.

"I saw today," Signor Naccarelli began in measured

tones, but when Mrs. Johnson suddenly sneezed, "Why did not you tell me?" he burst out, turning on her. "What can you be thinking of?"

Stricken silent, she walked on beside him. Somehow, then, he had found out. Certain dreary, familiar feelings returned to her. Meeting Noel at the airport, Clara behind in the car, wronged again, poor little victim of her own or her mother's impulses. Well, if Signor Naccarelli was to be substituted for Noel, she thought with relief that anyway she should at last confess. Instead of Bermuda, they could go to the first boat sailing from Naples.

"It is too much," went on Signor Naccarelli. "Two, three years, where there is love, where there is agreement, I say it is all right. But no, it is too much. It is to make the fantastic."

"Years?" she repeated.

"Can it be possible! But you must have understood! My son Fabrizio is twenty years old, no more. Whereas, your daughter, I see with my two eyes, written in the passport today in the office of the parroco: twenty-six! Six years difference! It cannot be. In that moment I ask myself, What must I say, what can I do? Soon it will be too late. What to do? I make the excuse, an appointment. I see often in the cinema this same excuse. It was not true. I have lied. I tell you frankly."

"I had not thought of her being older," said Mrs. Johnson. Weak with relief, she stopped walking. When she leaned her elbow against the parapet, she felt it trembling.

"Believe me, Signor Naccarelli, they seemed so much the same age to me, it had not entered my mind that there was any difference."

"It cannot be," said Signor Naccarelli positively, scowling out toward the noble skyline of his native city. "I pass an afternoon of torment, an inferno. As I am a man, as I am a Florentine, as I am a father, as I long for my son's happiness, as—" Words failed him.

"But surely the difference between them is not as great as that," Mrs. Johnson reasoned. "In America we have seen many, many happy marriages with an even greater difference. Clara—she has been very carefully brought up; she had a long illness some years ago. To me she seemed even younger than Fabrizio."

"A long illness." He whirled on her scornfully. "How am I to know that she is cured of it?"

"You see her," countered Mrs. Johnson. "She is as healthy as she seems."

"It cannot be." He turned away.

"Don't you realize," Mrs. Johnson pleaded, "that they are in love? Whatever their ages are, they are both young. This is a deep thing, a true thing. To try to stop what is between them now—"

"*Try* to stop? My dear lady, I will stop whatever I wish to stop."

"Fabrizio—" she began.

"Yes, yes. He will try to kill himself. It is only to grow up. I also have sworn to take my life—can you believe?

97

With passion I shake like this—and here I am today. No, no. To talk is one thing, to do another. Do not make illusions. He will not."

"But Clara—" she began. Her voice faltered. She thought she would cry in spite of herself.

Signor Naccarelli scowled out toward the dark river. "It cannot be," he repeated.

Mrs. Johnson looked at him and composure returned to her. Because whether this was comedy or tragedy, he had told her the truth. He could and would stop everything if he chose, and Fabrizio would not kill himself. If Mrs. Johnson had thought it practical, she would have murdered Signor Naccarelli. Instead, she suggested that they cross over to a small bar. She was feeling that perhaps a brandy. . . .

The bar was a tourist trap, placed near to American Express and crowded during the day. At night few people wandered in. Only one table was occupied at present. In the far corner what looked to Mrs. Johnson exactly like a girl from Winston-Salem was conversing with an American boy who was growing a beard. Mrs. Johnson chose a table at equidistance between the pair and the waiter. She gave her order and waited, saying nothing till the small glass on the saucer was set before her. It was her last chance and she knew it. It helped her timing considerably to know how much she detested Signor Naccarelli.

 "This is all too bad," said Mrs. Johnson softly. "I received a letter from my husband today. Instead of five thousand dollars, he wants to make Clara and Fabrizio a present of fifteen thousand dollars."

"That is nine million three hundred and seventy-five thousand lire," said Signor Naccarelli. "So now you will write and explain everything, and that this wedding cannot be."

"Yes," said Mrs. Johnson and sipped her brandy.

Presently Signor Naccarelli ordered a cup of coffee.

Later on they might have been observed in various places, strolling about quiet, less frequented streets. Their talk ran on many things. Signor Naccarelli recalled her sneeze, and wondered if she were cold. Mrs. Johnson was busily working out in the back of her mind how she was going to get fifteen thousand dollars without her husband, for the moment, knowing anything about it. It would take most of a family legacy, invested in her own name; and the solemn confidence of a lawyer, an old family friend; a long-distance request for him to trust her and cooperate; a promise that Noel would know everything anyway, within the month. Later, explaining to Noel: "In the U.S., you would undoubtedly have wanted to build a new house for your daughter and her husband. . . ." A good point.

"You must forgive me," said Signor Naccarelli, "if I ask a most personal thing of you. The Signorina Clara, she would like to have children, would she not? My wife can think of nothing else."

"Oh, Clara longs for children!" said Mrs. Johnson.

Toward midnight, they stopped in a bar for a final brandy. Signor Naccarelli insisted on paying, as always.

When she returned to her room, Margaret Johnson sat on her bed for a while, then she stood at the window for a

99

while and looked down on the river. With one finger, she touched her mouth where there lingered an Italian kiss.

How had she maneuvered herself out of further, more prolonged, and more intimately staged embraces without giving the least impression that she hadn't enjoyed the one he had surprised her with? In the shadow of a handsome façade, before the stout, lion-mouth crested arch where he had beckoned her to stop— "Something here will interest you, perhaps"—how, oh how, had she managed to manage it well? Out of practice in having to for, she shuddered to think, how many years. Nor could anything erase, remove from her the estimable flash of his eye, so near her own, so near.

"Mother!"

Why, I had forgotten *her*, thought Mrs. Johnson.

"Yes, darling, I'm coming!" In Clara's room she switched on a dim Italian lamp. "There, now, it's all going to be all right. We're going to meet them tomorrow, just as we did today. But tomorrow it will be all right. Go to sleep now. You'll see."

It's true, she thought, smoothing Clara's covers, switching out the light. No doubt of it now. And to keep down the taste of success, she bit hard on her lip (so lately kissed). If he let me out so easily, it means he doesn't want to risk anything. It means he wants this wedding. He wants it too.

xiii

IN THAT AFTERNOON's gentle decline, Fabrizio had found himself restless and irritable. Earlier, he had deliberately ignored his promise to meet Giuseppe, who was doubtless burning to find out why the luncheon had not come off. That day he travelled unfamiliar paths, did not return home for lunch, and spent the siesta hours sulking about the Boboli Gardens, where an unattractive American lady with a guide-book flattered herself that he was pursuing her. Every emotion seemed stronger than usual. If anyone he knew should see him here! He all but dashed out at the thought, entered narrow streets, and in a poor quarter gnawed a workingman's sandwich—a hard loaf with a paper-thin slice of salami. When the black cloud blew up he waited in the door of a church he had never seen before.

About six he entered his own little shop, where he had been seldom seen of late and then always full of jokes and laughter. Now he asked for the books and, finding that some handkerchief boxes had got among the gloves, imagined that everything was in disorder and that the cousin was busy ruining his business and robbing him. The cousin, who had been robbing him, but only mildly (they both understood almost to the lire exactly how much), insisted that Fabrizio should pay him his wages at once and he would leave and never return voluntarily as long as he lived. They both became bored with the argument.

Fabrizio thought of Clara. When he thought of her thighs and breasts he sighed; weakness swept him; he grew almost ill. So he thought of her face instead: gentle, beautiful, it rose before him. He saw it everywhere, that face. No lonely villa on a country hillside, yellow in the sun, oleanders on the terrace, but might have inside a chapel, closed off, unused for years, but on the wall a fresco, work of some ancient name known in all the world, a lost work—Clara. He loved her. She looked up at him now out of the glass-enclosed counter for merchandise, but the face was only his own, framed in socks.

At evening, at dark, he went the opposite way from home, down the Arno, walking sometimes along the streets, descending wherever he could to walk along the bank itself. He saw the sun set along the flow, and stopping in the dark at last he said aloud, "I could walk to Pisa." At another direction into the dark, he said, "Or Vallombrosa." Then he turned, ascended the bank to the road and walked back home. Possessed by an even deeper mood, the strangest he had ever known, he wandered about the city, listening to the echo of his own steps in familiar streets and looking at towering shapes of stone. The night seemed to be moving along secretly, but fast; the earth, bearing all burdens lightly, spinning and racing ahead—just as a Florentine had said, so it did. The silent towers tilted toward the dawn.

He saw his father the next morning. "It is all right," said Signor Naccarelli. "I have talked a long time with the signora. We will go today as yesterday to the office of the parroco."

"But Papà!" Fabrizio spread all ten fingers wide and shook his hands violently before him. "You had me sick with worry. My heart almost stopped. Yesterday I was like a crazy person. I have never spent such a day."

"Yes, well. I am sorry. The signorina is a bit older than I thought. Not much, but— Did you know?"

"Of course I knew. I told you so. Long ago. Did you forget it?"

"Perhaps I did. Never mind. And you, my son. You are twenty-one years, vero?"

"Papà!" Here Fabrizio all but left the earth itself. "I am twenty-three! The sun has cooked your brain. I should be the one to act like this."

"All right, all right. I was mistaken. But my instinct

103

was right." He tapped his brow. "It is always better to discuss everything in great detail. I felt that we were going
too quickly. You cannot be too careful in these things. But
my son—" He caught the boy's shoulder. "Remember to say
nothing to the Americans. Do you want them to think we
are crazy?"

"You are innamorato of the signora. I understand it
all."

xiv

AT THE WEDDING Margaret Johnson sat quietly while a
dream unfolded before her. She watched closely and missed
nothing.

She saw Clara emerge like a fresh flower out of the
antique smell of candle smoke, incense and damp stone,
and advance in white Venetian lace with so deep a look
shadowing out the hollow of her cheek, she might have
stood double for a Botticelli. As for Fabrizio, he who had
such a gift for appearing did not fail them. His beauty was
outshone only by his outrageous pride in himself; he saw
to it that everybody saw him well. Like an angel appearing
in a painting, he seemed to face outward to say, This is

105

what I look like, see? But his innocence protected him like magic.

Clara lifted her veil like a good girl exactly when she had been told to. Fabrizio looked at her and love sprang up in his face. The priest went on intoning, and since it was twelve o'clock all the bells from over the river and nearby began to ring at slightly different intervals—the deep-throated ones and the sweet ones, muffled and clear—one could hear them all.

The Signora Naccarelli had come into her own that day. She obviously believed that she had had difficulties to overcome in bringing about this union, but having got the proper heavenly parties well-informed, she had brought everything into line. Her bosom had sometimes been known to heave and her eye to dim, but that day she was serene. She wore flowers and an enormous medallion of her dead mother outlined in pearls. That unlikely specimen, a middle-class Neapolitan, she now seemed both peasant and goddess. Her hair had never been more smoothly bound, and natural color touched her large cheeks. Before the wedding, the wicked Giuseppe had seen her and run into her arms. Smiling perpetually at no one, it was as though she had created them all.

Signor Naccarelli had escorted Margaret Johnson to her place and sat beside her. He kept his arms tightly folded across his chest, and his face wore an odd, unreadable expression, mouth somewhat pursed, his high, cold, Florentine nose drawn toughly across the bridge. Perhaps his collar was too tight.

Yes, Margaret Johnson saw everything, even the only

person to cry, Giuseppe's wife, who had chosen to put her sophisticated self into a girlish, English-type summer frock of pale blue with a broad white collar.

I will not be needed any more, thought Margaret Johnson with something like a sigh, for before her eyes the strongest maternal forces in the world were taking her daughter to themselves. I have stepped out of the picture forever, she thought, and as if to bear her out, as the ceremony ended and everyone started moving toward the church door, no one noticed Margaret Johnson at all. They were waiting to form the wedding cortege which would wind over the river and up the hill to the restaurant and the long luncheon.

She did not mind not being noticed. She had done her job, and she knew it. She had played single-handed and unadvised a tricky game in a foreign country, and she had managed to realize from it the dearest wish of her heart. Signora Naccarelli was passing—one had to pause until the suction of that lady in motion had faded. Then Mrs. Johnson moved through the atrium and out to the colonnaded porch where, standing aside from the others, she could observe Clara stepping into a car, her white skirts dazzling in the sun. Clara saw her mother: they waved to one another. Fabrizio was made to wave as well. Over everybody's head a bronze fountain in the piazza jetted water into the sunlight, and nearby a group of tourists had stopped to look.

Clara and Fabrizio were driving off. So it had really happened! It was done. Mrs. Johnson found her vision blotted out. The reason was simply that Signor Naccarelli, that old devil, had come between her and whatever she was looking at; now he was smiling at her. The money again. There it was, forever returning, the dull moment of exchange.

Who was fooling whom? she longed to say, but did not. Or rather, since we both had our little game to play, which of us came off better? Let's tell the truth at last, you and I.

It was a great pity, Signor Naccarelli was saying, that Signor Johnson could not have been here to see so beautiful a wedding. Mrs. Johnson agreed.

Though no one knew it but herself, Signor Johnson at that very moment was winging his way to Rome. She had cut things rather fine; it made her shudder to realize how close a schedule she had had to work with. Tomorrow she would rise early to catch the train to Rome, to wait at the airport for Noel to land, but wait alone this time, and, no matter what he might think or say, triumphant.

He was going to think and say a lot, Noel Johnson was, and she knew she had to brace herself. He was going to go on believing for the rest of his life, for instance, that she had bought this marriage, the way American heiresses used to engage obliging titled gentlemen as husbands. No use telling him that sort of thing was out of date. Was money ever out of date, he would want to know?

But Margaret Johnson was going to weather the storm with Noel, or so at any rate she had the audacity to believe. Hadn't he in some mysterious way already, at what point she did not know, separated his own life from that of his daughter's? A defective thing must go: she had seen him act upon this principle too many times not to feel that in some fundamental, unconscious way he would, long ago, have broken this link. Why had he done so? Why, indeed? Why are we all and what are we really doing? Who was to say when *he*, in turn, had irritated the selfish, greedy nature of things and been kicked on the head in all the joyousness of his playful ways? No, it would be pride alone that was going to make him angry: she had gone behind his back. At least so she believed.

Though weary of complexities and more than ready to take a long rest from them all, Mrs. Johnson was prepared on the strength of her belief to make one more gamble yet, namely, that however Noel might rage, no honeymoon was going to be interrupted, that Signor Naccarelli was not going to be searched out and told the truth, and that the officials of the great Roman Church could sleep peacefully in rich apartments or poor damp cells, undisturbed by Noel Johnson. He would grow quiet at last, and in the quiet, even Margaret Johnson had not yet dared to imagine what sort of life, what degree of delight in it, they might not be able to discover (rediscover?) together. This was uncertain. What was certain was that in that same quiet she would begin to miss her daughter. She would go on missing her forever.

She was swept by a strange weakness. Signor Naccarelli was offering her his arm, but she could not move to take it. Her head was spinning and she leaned instead against the cool stone column. She did not feel able to move. Beyond them, the group of tourists were trying to take a picture, but were unable to shield their cameras from the light's terrible strength. A scarf was tried, a coat; would some person cast a shadow?

"Do you remember," it came to Mrs. Johnson to ask Signor Naccarelli, "the man who fell down when the cannon fired that day? What happened to him?"

"He died," said Signor Naccarelli.

She saw again, as if straight into her vision, painfully contracting it, the flash that the sun had all but blurred away to nothing. She heard again the momentary hush under heaven, followed by the usual noise's careless resumption. In desperate motion through the flickering rhythms of the "event," he went on and on in glimpses, trying to get up, while near him, silent in bronze, Cellini's Perseus, in the calm repose of triumph, held aloft the Medusa's head.

"I did the right thing," she said. "I know I did."

Signor Naccarelli made no reply. 'The right thing': what was it?

Whatever it was, it was a comfort to Mrs. Johnson, who presently felt strong enough to take his arm and go with him, out to the waiting car.

THE END

110

ABOUT THE AUTHOR

ELIZABETH SPENCER was born in Carrollton, Mississippi, in 1921 and has been writing fiction since early childhood. After graduation from Belhaven College in 1942, she took an M.A. in English at Vanderbilt University the following year. For the next two years she taught English at a school for girls in Nashville, then became a reporter for the NASH-VILLE TENNESSEAN.

Miss Spencer's first novel, *Fire in the Morning*, was published in 1948, and was declared by THE NEW YORK TIMES BOOK REVIEW one of the three best first novels of that year. Her second, *This Crooked Way*, appeared in 1952, while she was teaching creative writing at the University of Mississippi. In 1953 the author received a Guggenheim Fellowship and went to Italy for two years, living principally in Florence and Rome. Her third novel, *The Voice at the Back Door* (McGraw-Hill, 1956), received notable critical success, including the Rosenthal Award of the National Institute of Arts and Letters, and the Kenyon Review Fiction Fellowship. Its commercial success included translation into a number of foreign languages, release in reprint form in both America and Great Britain, and sale to the motion pictures.

Miss Spencer was married in 1956 to John Rusher of Cornwall, England, whom she met in Italy. They now live near Montreal. One of her recent *New Yorker* stories, "First Dark," was included in *Prize Stories, 1960: The O. Henry Awards*. The present work, *The Light in the Piazza*, was also written in Canada.